Trust was dange

He might find himsel
forgive her and risk
interest he should never have revealed in the
first place.

It would be a relief to finish this surgery. He
should have sent Sarah away to rest. He was
too aware of her standing so close. He could
even smell a faint scent of her—an occasional
waft of something fresh like a fruit-flavoured
shampoo that cut through the clinical smell of
the operating theatre.

He could sense every tiny movement she
made, and when their hands touched, as they
did now, with the passing of a fresh suture
needle and thread, Ben could feel the
astonishing tingle of her skin even through the
gloves.

Or was it just his skin that tingled?

Dear Reader

Stories only work when the characters become real to both the writer and you, the reader. The characters' pasts strongly influence the way they behave in the present, and some characters can be powerful enough to refuse to stay in the background for long. **A MOTHER FOR HIS FAMILY** is Sarah Mitchell's story.

But Sarah's foster-sister, Tori, refused to say in the background. She demanded a story of her own. You can find Tori's story soon in A NURSE'S SEARCH AND RESCUE from Mills & Boon® Medical Romance™ in September 2005:

Emergency nurse Tori is just looking for fun! She hopes to have kids of her own one day, but not yet—and the idea of taking on somebody else's? No way! So, no matter how gorgeous Dr Matthew Buchanan is, his four orphaned nieces and nephews are a big no-no—aren't they…?

Sarah Mitchell and Tori Preston are foster-sisters, best friends and fellow nurses. They're as different in personality as they are in looks. These two women shared so much in the past, but have very different issues now, affecting their lives and their relationships with the men they love.

I hope you enjoy their stories and share the happiness they both eventually find.

With love

Alison Roberts

A MOTHER FOR HIS FAMILY

BY
ALISON ROBERTS

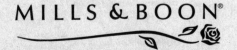

*All the characters in this book have no existence outside the imagination
of the author, and have no relation whatsoever to anyone bearing the
same name or names. They are not even distantly inspired by any
individual known or unknown to the author, and all the incidents are
pure invention.*

*First published in Great Britain 2005
Harlequin Mills & Boon Limited,
Eton House, 18-24 Paradise Road, Richmond, Surrey TW9 1SR*

© Alison Roberts 2005

ISBN 0 263 84317 3

*Set in Times Roman 10½ on 12 pt.
03-0705-45937*

*Printed and bound in Spain
by Litografia Rosés, S.A., Barcelona*

CHAPTER ONE

'*YES!*'

Sarah Mitchell was only on page ten of the romantic saga she had found in the airport bookshop but already she was hooked. Her companion's exclamation was startling, to say the least, and Sarah's response was wary.

'*Yes*, what?'

'That's *him*.'

'Who?'

'The father of my children.'

'Oh, *no*!' Reluctantly, Sarah closed her book. Her eyelids temporarily followed suit as she sighed. 'Tori, it was *your* idea to come here for a break, remember?'

'To have fun,' Tori agreed happily. 'Something you don't get nearly enough of.'

'A winter escape,' Sarah continued. 'Sun, sand and surf. Sex was not on the agenda. We *agreed*!'

'That was before it climbed out of that boat.'

'What climbed out?' Sarah opened her eyes and pushed herself up on her elbows. It was only 10 a.m. but already hot enough for the turquoise expanse of the sea to look extremely inviting.

'The most gorgeous man I've ever seen in my life. *Look!*'

The landing jetty for the Fijian island resort was not too far down the beach. The man who had climbed out of the small boat was now standing in

5

ankle-deep water with several small children hanging onto his hands.

'He likes kids,' Tori pronounced gleefully.

'He's probably got six of his own. Like Robert.'

'Robert only had two.'

'And a wife to go with them. One that he wasn't going to bother telling you about, remember?'

'Yeah…' Tori sighed and then shook her head. 'That was months ago. I'm over it.' She flashed a grin at Sarah. 'Life *does* go on, you know.'

The sparkle was irresistible and Sarah had to smile back. Heavens, they'd had little enough to smile about over the last year, hadn't they? What harm could there be in enjoying a little eye candy?

They both watched as the man accepted a large hibiscus flower from an older child. He pushed the stalk of the vibrant orange bloom through thick waves of dark hair to anchor it behind his left ear.

'The left ear,' Tori breathed. 'That's supposed to signify availability, isn't it?'

'I think it only applies to women,' Sarah countered. 'And anyway he's not an islander.'

'He seems to know everyone. I wonder who he is?'

'Looks like a pilot.' Sarah had to admit it was hard to look away from the expanse of lean, tanned limbs showing around the uniform-like pale shorts and an open-necked, short-sleeved shirt that had a tropical pattern to rival the hibiscus bloom. 'Or maybe he drives one of those tourist launches.'

'I think we should book a day trip.'

'We only just got here yesterday! I want to lie on the beach and soak up some sun.' Sarah rolled to lean on one elbow and reached for the satisfyingly thick paperback beside her towel. 'I'll go for a swim every time I get too hot reading my book.'

Tori made a sound that could have been a growl. Then it turned into a squeak. 'He's coming this way! Help!'

'Just smile and bat your eyelashes,' Sarah muttered. 'Seems to work for you most times.'

She wasn't jealous. She loved Tori enough to be thankful that she was young and attractive, vivacious and determined to enjoy life. That courage had pulled Sarah away from some of the bleakness of the last few months. 'Mum hated to see people unhappy,' she had reminded Sarah gently. 'I'll bet she's watching you right now and making those "tch-tch" noises.'

Sometimes a little of that bounce even rubbed off onto Sarah and let her do something expensively self-indulgent, like taking a week's holiday on a tropical island in the middle of winter.

She hoped she hadn't sounded jealous. Or older-sister crusty. But, for heaven's sake, Tori needed someone to watch out for her. That romance with Robert had been a total disaster and just too much to handle on top of Mum's death. The desire to see a little of Tori's sparkle return had been the deciding factor to her agreeing to this holiday, but a sparkle associated with another man was the last thing Tori needed.

'Morning, ladies. Lovely day for it.'

It would be too rude to keep pretending to read her book. Sarah peered over the top of her sunglasses and got the full blast of the man at very close quarters as he slowed his progress along the beach to a halt.

'Perfect!' Tori was smiling broadly and Sarah knew it wasn't just the weather she was praising.

'Just arrived?'

'Yesterday.'

'Enjoying yourselves?'

'It just keeps getting better.'

Sarah disguised the twitch of her lips by smiling at the more serious-looking older boy who seemed to be guarding a large fishing-tackle kit.

'*Bula.*'

She was rewarded for using the island greeting by a chorus of responses and gleaming grins on small, dark faces, but the girl holding one of the man's hands in both of hers buried her face with its halo of fuzzy dark curls against the pale shorts.

Sarah's smile softened and she glanced up, wondering if the man was aware of his small companion's shyness. The instant answer she found in a pair of very dark eyes was disconcerting. The way he swung the child up into his arms and kissed her cheek gently as he gave her a cuddle was utterly charming. He settled her onto one hip and there was a slight scuffle as the other children raced to claim his free hand.

'Better go,' he said. 'Have a great holiday.'

'Thanks, we will,' Sarah said politely.

'You, too!' Tori called after him.

He laughed. 'Some of us are here to work, not play.' He turned his head a few steps later and he was still smiling. 'Tough job,' he said sternly, 'but, hey! Someone's gotta do it.'

Water slid over her skin like the touch of satin sheets on an overly hot summer's night. Waves, too lazy to break until they reached the shore, rocked her gently and tiny, brightly coloured fish darted through the crystal clarity of the shallows like jewels.

'This is bliss,' Sarah sighed happily. 'Seven whole days of absolute paradise. I'm so glad you talked me into this, Tori.'

'We should go and get some lunch.'

'It's only eleven o'clock. The restaurant won't be open yet.'

'You can get snacks any time and I'm *starving*!'

'Get one of the islanders to knock a coconut down for you. Look, there's someone near our bure right now.'

Sarah waved towards the thatched hut, set amongst the coconut palms only a stone's throw from the beach, aware of yet another contented smile pulling at her lips. While the hut looked primitive and totally in keeping with the setting from the outside, the interior could only be described as luxurious. Even the huge gecko attached to their ceiling by its sticky feet hadn't distracted them from admiring the furnishings and bathroom facilities or enjoying the champagne and basket of tropical fruit awaiting their arrival.

Tori stood up, water flowing from the red bikini that covered her curves. She shook her head, releasing a spray of droplets from her curly blonde hair.

'*He'd* know, wouldn't he?'

'About coconuts? Sure.'

'No, about that man. Who he is. He *said* he worked here, didn't he?'

'Well, he said he was here to work. I'm not sure that's quite the same thing.'

'Maybe he's a film director checking out a new location.'

'Or a novelist, trying to find a quiet spot to finish off his latest bestseller.'

'Maybe he *owns* this resort!' Tori's eyes widened

dramatically as she considered the fabulous possibilities. Then she made a decisive move towards the beach, swooping to collect her towel and sunglasses. 'I'll find out,' she announced. 'Watch this space!'

The space didn't stay empty for long. Tori was back within minutes, splashing excitedly through the shallows and then wading in to where Sarah was floating on her back.

'He's a *doctor*!' she reported breathlessly. '"Doctor Ben", they call him. He's come to see one of the women in the village. Sounds like she's having a baby any day now.'

'So that's why that boy was carrying the kit. I thought it was a bit odd to have fishing tackle and no rod.'

'I asked if there was a "Mrs Ben", but I don't think he understood.' Tori was frowning. 'That was when he started talking about the "missus" in the village who's having a baby.'

'Why don't you sprain your ankle or something? Just in time for when he comes back along the beach.'

Tori appeared to give the tongue-in-cheek suggestion serious thought but then laughed.

'I think going to the restaurant is a much better idea. We can see the boats from the deck by that pool. He might even have lunch there himself.' Tori was off again. 'I'm going to get changed and do something with my hair!'

It didn't matter what route they chose to take. Paths that meandered beneath the palms, between accommodation and service bures, past a chapel and even a tiny fire station, eventually all led to the central complex that was the resort's hub. Neither did it matter how long it took to get there. They were on island time now and Sarah had actually taken off her watch and dropped it into her suitcase when she'd gone inside to shower after her swim.

The sense of escaping more than just a timetable was heady. The atmosphere of this tropical playground offered the promise of finding whatever they might be searching for. They could choose the peace of simply soaking up the sunshine, lazing in water just cool enough to be refreshing or strolling along walkways shaded by exotic trees. Or they could go for the excitement of scuba-diving, windsurfing or parasailing. Right now, peace was something Sarah craved. Time out after a tough year.

The cry that interrupted their ambling progress past the turtle nursery was anything but peaceful.

'What on earth was that?'

'Sounds like someone's been hurt.'

'Where did it come from?'

'Just over there.' Sarah was already moving, heading away from the path and through a thick clump of hibiscus bushes. 'I think it's the miniature golf course.'

An elderly woman was lying on the ground. Her companion was holding her hand.

'Marjorie! Are you all right, darling?'

'Hi. My name's Sarah. I'm a nurse. Can I help?'

'She fell over. Marjorie?'

'I'm fine, Stanley. Don't fuss.' The woman was struggling to sit up.

'Does anything hurt?'

'I don't think so. Help me up, Stanley.' Marjorie held up her hands but cried out as she tried to stand up. 'My ankle! *Ah-h!*'

'Let's sit her down,' Sarah instructed. 'On that turtle.' She looked up to engage Tori's assistance as she helped support the woman, but to her surprise she was alone with the elderly couple. Tori must have gone to find help, she decided. And suddenly her absence wasn't so surprising. Sarah could guess precisely whose help she would be seeking.

The large concrete turtle crouching over one of the target holes for the golf course made an excellent seat. Sarah was pleased to see some colour returning to Marjorie's cheeks.

'Damn and blast!' the woman exclaimed. 'I *knew* these sandals were going to be trouble.'

'Does anything else hurt?' Sarah asked. 'Did you hit your head when you fell?'

'Would take more than concrete to knock Marj out,' Stanley said.

Sarah smiled. 'Can you remember what happened? Were you feeling unwell in any way before you fell?'

'No, I'm as fit as a fiddle. It was these sandals. I came down that hill too fast and turned my foot.'

'She was excited,' Stanley explained. 'She got a hole in one under that turtle.'

'I did, didn't I?' Marjorie beamed at Stanley. 'Not so dusty for an old girl, huh?'

Sarah's smile widened. 'How old *are* you, Marjorie?'

'Seventy-seven.' Marjorie leaned towards Sarah. 'Stanley's only sixty-eight. Take my advice, sweetie. Always go for a younger man.'

'We're on our honeymoon,' Stanley added proudly. 'We got married here, on the beach.'

'Oh, how lovely! I've always thought that a tropical island wedding would be just perfect.'

'It was.' Marjorie nodded. 'Until now.' She groaned. 'Do you think I've broken it?'

'Let's have a look.' Sarah eased a sandal with a high cork sole from Marjorie's foot.

Stanley was holding Marjorie's hand again and looking very anxious. They both watched as Sarah carefully examined the foot and ankle.

'Can you wiggle your toes?'

Brightly painted toenails waggled a little feebly.

'Try moving the whole foot.'

'Ouch!' Marjorie exclaimed. Then she tried again. 'It's not so bad,' she decided.

'I don't think anything's broken,' Sarah told her finally. 'It looks like a sprain to me. What we need is some ice and a bandage and somewhere for Marjorie to put her foot up for a while.'

Marjorie's face creased with disappointment. 'But we were going to go snorkelling this afternoon.'

'See how it feels a bit later.' Sarah stood up. 'I'll see if I can find someone to help. I believe there's a doctor on the island at the moment, in fact.'

'That wouldn't be him, would it?'

Stanley pointed past her shoulder in the direction of the turtle pond and it didn't really surprise Sarah at all to see Tori coming towards them with 'Doctor Ben' in tow. The boy carrying the kit was still with him but the other children had vanished.

Tori looked very happy. 'This is Ben Dawson, Sarah. He's a doctor. Wasn't it lucky I spotted him after we heard that screaming?'

'I didn't scream,' Marjorie protested. 'I never scream, do I, Stanley?'

'You came pretty close the other night,' Stanley murmured.

'Stanley!'

'This is Marjorie, Dr Dawson.' Sarah was struggling to keep a straight face and Tori's smothering of a giggle was not entirely successful. 'She tripped over and turned her ankle. No prior symptoms and she doesn't appear to have injured anything else.'

'Call me Ben.' Dark eyes were twinkling as Ben made no serious attempt to hide his enjoyment of this scene. 'You got married the other day, didn't you, Marjorie?'

'Sure did, Doctor. Best thing that's happened to me in a few decades.'

'I saw the wedding from a distance,' Ben said. 'Gorgeous dress.' He smiled at Stanley. 'I liked the white suit, too. Perfect choice for a beach wedding.'

'We've only got two days of our honeymoon left,' Marjorie told him. 'Sarah says my ankle's not broken and she's a nurse so she should know, shouldn't she?'

'Absolutely.' Ben smiled at Sarah and then turned to include Tori in the group. 'This is Sarah's friend, Tori, and she's a nurse as well. You've just about got a whole emergency department here. Isn't that lucky?'

Marjorie didn't seem overly impressed. 'I don't need a department. I need to know that I can go snorkelling this afternoon.

'I suggested ice,' Sarah said. 'And a bandage and elevation—at least for a while.'

'Sounds like good advice to me. How 'bout I check that ankle out?' His glance at Sarah looked suspiciously like a wink. 'A second opinion can't hurt, can it?'

Oh, he was charming all right. How many doctors would be prepared to simply back up the diagnosis of a nurse? He was doing exactly what he should be doing as a more highly qualified professional but he was managing to make it seem like an unnecessary formality.

'RICE,' he pronounced a short time later. 'Rest, ice, compression and elevation.'

'Exactly what Sarah said.' Stanley nodded. 'Except for that compression bit.'

'That's the bandage,' Ben told him. 'And I expect my assistant, Josefa, knows just where to find one.'

The lanky teenager's face lit up in a grin. The kit was open in a flash and three sizes of bandage were produced for Ben to choose from. Josefa ran off just as eagerly when Ben explained the need for an ice pack. Tori supported Marjorie's ankle while Ben did an expert job of the bandaging. Sarah wondered if he noticed, as she did, how often Tori's hand seemed to get just a little in the way.

'Now, let's get you back to your bure for a rest,' Ben declared finally. To Marjorie's evident delight, he effortlessly picked the elderly woman up in his arms.

'I've been swept off my feet,' she cried happily.

'I thought I did that,' Stanley grumbled.

'It's OK, Stanley.' Ben grinned. 'I'm not half as handsome as you and I promise I'll give her back. Now, which direction is your bure?'

'Oh, no, you don't,' Marjorie said firmly. 'I might have to sit but I'm not going to waste the rest of my day. I want to sit by the pool where I can look at something more interesting than my foot.'

'We could have some lunch.'

'And champagne, Stanley. Don't forget we're on our honeymoon.'

'Lunch sounds like an excellent idea,' Ben said. 'I'm heading that way myself so I'll be able to keep an eye on you, Marjorie. I don't want to see you dancing on any of those tables.'

Marjorie actually giggled and Sarah fell back behind the group as she shook her head imperceptibly. Ben Dawson was clearly a hit with ladies of all ages. If she had been feeling unkind she would have labelled him a flirt but it was hard to feel unkind with the sunshine and warmth and laughter all around her.

Tori fell back to keep step with Sarah. 'Lunch,' she murmured. 'Told you my idea was the best.'

'It was the sprained ankle that worked,' Sarah whispered back. 'Just lucky it didn't have to be yours.'

'Yeah.' Tori laughed and her voice rose unconsciously. 'Nothing to stop me dancing on a table or two, is there?'

Stanley and Ben both turned. Both men had an identical appreciative expression and Sarah almost groaned aloud.

'I sincerely hope you won't,' she muttered.

'Don't worry.' Tori ducked to sweep up some hibiscus blooms lying beneath a nearby bush. 'I'm far too hungry.' She handed one of the flowers to Sarah and then poked another behind her ear.

'Is it the left ear if you're single?' she asked nobody in particular.

'Couldn't say for sure,' Ben responded. 'But I think that's how it goes.'

'You've lost yours,' Tori told him. 'Would you like another?'

'Sure.' Ben's pause allowed Tori to stand on tiptoe and position the flower.

'On the left for you, too?'

'Absolutely.'

He turned to cast a meaningful look at the flower Sarah held. She blushed, trying to wipe off any 'here we go again' expression she had been unconsciously adopting as she watched Tori. She poked the stalk of her bloom through a buttonhole on her soft shirt, the tails of which she had knotted loosely around her waist.

'Ah…a woman of mystery,' Ben said.

'Keep it that way, honey,' Marjorie piped up from his arms. 'Keep 'em guessing and you'll keep 'em interested.'

The laughter covered what could have been an embarrassing moment and then they were in the main complex. Josefa was waiting, having gathered a bag of ice from the bar. A lounge chair was found, as well as cushions to raise Marjorie's foot, a matching chair for Stanley and a bottle of complimentary champagne from a resort manager who was upset to learn of the accident.

Finally Sarah and Tori were settled at a table shaded by a bougainvillea-draped pergola, plates piled high with samples of the chargrilled chicken and fish from the outdoor barbecues and a range of the most delicious-looking salads. The view was just as enticing, with the pergola framing a section of the lagoon where a group of new arrivals was being welcomed with necklaces of tropical flowers and a traditional song with a guitar accompaniment.

'Mind if I join you?'

Tori, her mouth full of chicken, kicked Sarah under the table.

'Please, do,' she said politely to Ben.

He sat down, immediately spearing a mouthful of perfectly grilled fish from his plate. 'Mmm,' he said, seconds later. 'You made the right choice of resort. They have the best cooks here.'

'Do you cover all the resorts?' Tori queried.

Ben shook his head. 'I happen to live quite close to this one so I've become a kind of honorary GP. I do visit a few islands that have larger villages to run the occasional clinic and I'm on call for emergencies, of course.'

'Like sunburn?' Sarah wished she had kept her mouth shut as Ben flicked her a surprised glance.

'It's quite easy to get seriously burnt in this climate,' he said. 'I hope you're both being careful.'

'You weren't here for an emergency today, though, were you?' Tori was clearly making an effort to distract Ben from any acidity Sarah's comment might have contained.

'No. I'm popping in every day to keep an eye on a patient whose blood pressure needs monitoring.'

'The one due to have the baby?'

Ben looked surprised again. 'How did you know that?'

'We heard about you.' Tori sounded perfectly innocent but her smile suggested that the information had all been good.

Ben returned the smile. 'You have an advantage over me, then.' He ate in silence for a minute. 'So…tell me about you.'

The glance was intended to draw Sarah into the conversation and she was happy to comply.

'We're both nurses,' she reminded him. 'I'm in paediatrics and Tori's in the emergency department at the moment.'

'Where are you from?'

'New Zealand. Auckland.'

'The largest city, right?'

Sarah nodded. 'And you? You sound English.'

Ben mirrored her nod. 'I'm a Londoner through and through.'

'Bit of a change working here, then.'

'A dream job,' Tori declared. 'Do you need any nurses?'

Ben laughed. 'It's not all free lunches at luxury resorts. I do work a couple of days a week at a hospital in Suva.'

'But you don't live on the main island?'

'No. I have my own little beach.' For an instant, Ben's face was shuttered. Then he smiled at Tori. 'How long are you here for?'

'Only a week.' Tori wrinkled her nose. 'I have a feeling it's not going to be nearly long enough.'

'You'll just have to make the most of every minute.'

'Oh, I intend to.'

Sarah ate her way through a wonderful salad that combined mango and pawpaw with rice and some flavours she couldn't identify. She felt shut out already but she wasn't going to spoil Tori's fun. If she needed a holiday romance to make her happy, why not? Maybe the gorgeous Ben would actually turn out to be the love of her life and they would settle in their island paradise and live happily ever after.

Tuning back into the conservation at the table became unavoidable as Sarah realised that Tori was beginning to cover some rather personal ground.

'It was Sarah that mostly nursed Mum through the

last few weeks after the second stroke,' she was saying. 'So it was even harder on her.'

'I'm sorry to hear that.' Ben sounded very sincere
but then his tone changed. 'You two are *sisters*?'

Sarah met the curious glance defensively. Yes, she
was taller than Tori, her hair long, straight and dark
in contrast to bouncy blonde curls and her body lean
and lacking any attractive curves. And, yes, their per-
sonalities were just as different and Sarah was not
about to bare her soul or anything else to a stranger.

'Foster-sisters.' Tori seemed unaware of any warning signals Sarah was emanating. 'But it's been the
real thing for ever as far as I'm concerned. Sas came
to live with us when she was fourteen and I was
eight.' Tori's smile at Sarah was loving. 'I'd always
wanted an older sister I could annoy.' She laughed.
'I'm twenty-four now and I still manage to annoy
her.'

'Only sometimes,' Sarah said mildly. 'But I'm sure
Ben isn't interested in hearing the details of our family history.'

Her disapproval of sharing personal information
hadn't been masked as well as she'd thought but the
slightly awkward silence that fell was broken only
seconds later as a woman wearing a silky white sarong paused by their table.

'Ben! How lovely to see you again.' She laughed
at his obvious mental scramble. 'Lisa,' she supplied.
'I was here this time last year.'

'Ah…' Ben's face cleared. 'Sunburn.'

Lisa smiled. 'I hope I thanked you properly for
taking such good care of me.'

'Of course.' Ben cleared his throat, looking
vaguely uncomfortable.

Lisa was looking over the top of her sunglasses at Tori, and Sarah had a wild desire to laugh aloud. Was this one of last year's conquests eyeing up the competition?

She put down her fork, her appetite suddenly sated. OK, she probably couldn't stop Tori if she wanted to have a fling but she would have to make sure Tori didn't have any dreams about it being the real thing. Ben Dawson might be incredibly good looking and charming but he *was* a flirt. A playboy. A complete lightweight who had set himself up in a perfect playground with an enticingly large field of probably very willing playmates.

Sarah wanted no part of it. She especially didn't want someone like this knowing too much about *her*. Sympathy, however sincere it might be, concerning her appalling childhood would not be welcome. At least even Tori's trusting openness couldn't reveal everything. There had only ever been one person who had known all there was to know about her and sadly she had taken Sarah's secrets with her to her grave only six months ago.

The woman in the sarong had moved on now. Ben stood up.

'I've got a bit of housekeeping to do at the medical centre,' he excused himself. 'I'd better get on with it.'

'You've got a medical centre here?'

'Just a small one,' he responded to Tori. 'Would you like to see it?'

She nodded, pushing her chair back. 'Coming, Sas?'

Sarah shook her head. 'I might go and have a chat

to Marjorie and see how her ankle is doing. Then I intend to go and flop on the beach with my book.'

Tori turned back and Sarah knew that if she wanted company she only had to say so. However attracted Tori was to Ben Dawson, at present it was simply intended as fun. If Sarah needed her, there was no question of where her loyalties would lie.

So Sarah smiled encouragingly. 'You go,' she told Tori. 'You'll know where to find me later.'

'Are you sure you don't want to come?'

'Absolutely.' Sarah's use of the affirmation Ben seemed to prefer was deliberate.

Dark eyes regarded her with a quizzical expression but his smile was more than simply courteous. 'Nice meeting you, Sarah. And thanks for your help with Marjorie.'

'It was a pleasure.'

'Let's hope the rest of your holiday isn't interrupted by further medical dramas.'

'Or any other sort,' Sarah murmured.

'Indeed.' Ben held her gaze just long enough to let her know he had received her message. Then he turned to Tori and his easy grin surfaced again. He crooked his elbow. 'Shall we?'

'Absolutely.' Tori slid her arm through his, turned to give Sarah a gleeful glance and then they were gone, screened by the palms lining the pathway to the main building complex.

Sarah stood up slowly, oddly disappointed that her suspicions regarding Ben's integrity had been so readily confirmed. Then she shrugged inwardly. What business of hers was it, anyway? She wasn't her sister's keeper and spending some time alone would not detract in any way from her enjoyment of these surroundings. Sarah Mitchell had learned very early in life that her own company could be preferable at times.

She didn't *have* to be by herself right now, anyway. Shading her eyes, she gazed towards the pool.

'Yoohoo!' Marjorie raised a champagne flute in her direction. 'Over here, darling! We've saved a glass for you.'

CHAPTER TWO

'It's *you* he's interested in.'

Sarah snorted. 'Yeah, sure.'

'I'm serious.' Tori buried her spoon into the bowl of fruit salad she had chosen for dessert. 'Is that mango or pawpaw, do you think?' She popped it into her mouth without waiting for Sarah's opinion and sighed with pleasure. 'Mmm. Whatever it is, it's delicious.'

The dance floor of the resort's main restaurant was being taken over by a group of islanders as Sarah and Tori finished their dinner. Men crouched to one side, holding small drums, and the women lined up, barefoot. Grass skirts swirled and rustled as they moved and the garlands of tropical flowers in their hair and around their wrists and necks added vibrant colour to the scene. Sarah turned her chair so she could watch the performance and from the first unaccompanied notes of rich harmony as the group started singing she was utterly captivated.

The song was joyous, the faces smiling, but somewhere in the layers of harmony there was a poignant sound that recognised how suffering could contribute to happiness. Sarah had never heard anything like it and was moved almost to tears. Then the mood changed and the women stamped their feet to the beat of the drums. The music soared with the new tempo and it was impossible not to tap her feet and clap along with it.

It wasn't until she was clapping until her hands hurt at the end of the performance that Sarah noticed Tori's face.

'What's so funny?'

'You were practically dancing on the table, Sas.'

'I was not!'

'Yes, you were!' Tori was still grinning. 'If Ben had seen you just now he wouldn't think you were so uptight.' She stood up. 'Let's go for a walk on the beach. I want to see the last of that sunset.'

Sarah followed but she wasn't thinking about any sunsets. She had been ignoring Tori's odd comments about Ben ever since she had come back from her tour of the medical centre, but this one had touched a real nerve.

'Did he actually *say* he thought I was uptight?'

Tori nodded. 'He asked what your problem was—and if it was all men you didn't trust or just him in particular?'

Sarah chuckled. 'Both.' But her amusement faded rapidly. How could he have seen so much in such a short space of time? Especially when she *knew* how good she was at keeping things hidden. 'I hope you didn't spend your whole time together talking about me.'

'Enough to give me the distinct impression that it's not my company he would prefer. I'm happy to back off, Sas. Why don't you give him a chance?'

'Even if I was desperate for a man—which I'm *not*—he'd be the last one I'd choose.'

'Why?'

'He's not attractive.' If she said it firmly enough, she would believe it. Wouldn't she?

Tori certainly didn't. 'Oh, come on! He's *gor-*

geous! Kind of halfway between Tom Cruise and Mel Gibson, I thought.'

'Looks aren't everything. You should have learned that much from Robert.' Sarah stooped to pick up the sandals she had just kicked off. She wiggled her toes in the sand appreciatively. 'A cute body and a killer smile are purely surface attributes. They don't really count much as far as I'm concerned.'

'What does really count, then?'

'Kindness,' Sarah answered after a thoughtful pause. 'And intelligence.'

'Ben's kind. Look at how much those kids love him. And he's a doctor, for heaven's sake. He can't be stupid.'

'He's not a *real* doctor.' Sarah shook her head dismissively. 'Looking after sunburnt tourists at holiday resorts? It's a cop-out. Like working on a cruise ship or for a drug company. Doctors like that don't really want a career. They're in it for the social life and the status. Oh...*look*!'

Sarah was more than ready to change the subject. That odd feeling of being somehow let down returned every time she thought about Ben and his tropical island dream job. She was pointing now to make sure Tori turned her attention seawards. The final throes of a dramatic blood-red sunset were gilding the water and highlighting the silhouettes of smaller, surrounding islands. The perfect finishing touch was a replica sailing ship, just beginning to furl some of the huge sails as it made its way towards the jetty.

Tori sank down on the sand to sit beside Sarah, but she could enjoy the view and talk at the same time.

'I think you're wrong about Ben, Sas. I like him, I really do.'

'He's all yours, then,' Sarah said lightly. 'Think of him as part of the holiday package. An extra treat.'

'I'd rather you had the treat.'

'Why?' Sarah forgot the sunset for a moment as she caught the unspoken message. 'I'm OK, Tori. Maybe it has been two years since anyone's been interested in me but I'm not burning up with frustration here.'

'There's plenty of interest. There always has been. You just chase everyone away.'

Sarah was silent for a few seconds. This wasn't the kind of indignant 'all men are bastards' support she had come to rely on from Tori. She always started any relationship with the hope that this was going to be it, but she had clocked up enough experience now to know that they always turned to custard. The only variation was how long it took. Maybe Tori was right and it *was* her attitude that was at fault. It wasn't the kind of thought conducive to a happy holiday, however, so Sarah tried to make a joke about it.

'I only do that to save time,' she said. 'And pride. If I wait too long, they end up dumping me.'

'Maybe that's because they think you don't trust them.'

'I *don't* trust them.'

Tori reached out to touch Sarah's hand. 'I know you had some awful stuff to deal with when you were a kid and I know you've never wanted to talk about it—'

'It's in the past,' Sarah interrupted. 'I'm over it.'

Tori's blue eyes had darkened in the fading light. 'It might still be doing damage, you know. All men aren't really bastards, Sas. There's some really good ones out there, too.'

'I know that.'

'I want you to find one.'

'I will. One day.'

'I worry about you.'

'There's no need. Honestly. I'm fine.'

Tori sighed, her gaze on the horizon again. 'Mum always said that out of all the kids she fostered after Dad died, you were the one that had the most special place in her heart. She said it was you that made us into a whole family, not her.'

Sarah had to swallow the lump in her throat. She was going to miss Carol so much.

'A wee while ago,' Tori continued softly, 'while Mum could still talk, she told me to watch out for you. To try and help you find the person who could help you create a family of your own. She said you had so much love to share it would be a terrible waste if you shut yourself away again.'

The sunset was forgotten, too blurred by tears to be enjoyed any more. Tori squeezed Sarah's hand and they sat there in silence until the crimson faded to a soft peach and then pearl grey before the swift descent of darkness.

'I love it here,' Sarah said finally. By mutual consent they started walking back towards their bure. Their closeness allowed them to move on from a sad topic and cheer each other up with a perfect understanding of what had been shared and acknowledged. 'It's like stepping into a postcard. A little bit of fantasy.'

'Speaking of fantasy...' Tori smiled. 'Haven't yours ever included someone like Ben?'

'Of course they have.'

'Ooh. Do tell.'

'No way. Fantasies are strictly private. And they're *never* real…they can't be.'

'They *could* be,' Tori said persuasively.

Sarah shook her head. 'Reality never measures up. Sex is overrated.'

'You've never been in love properly, that's all.'

'Nobody ever hangs around long enough for that to happen.'

It was Tori's turn to do the head-shaking. 'If you have to wait that long, or try and force it, then it's not going to happen. You're trying the wrong person. I think it—or at least the definite possibility of it—happens right from the first moment you see them.'

'Like Ben?'

'Oh, yes. He'd be very easy to fall in love with. That's why I think he'd be good for you.'

'Why would I want to fall in love with someone I'm only going to be around for a week?'

'Practice.' Tori grinned. 'That way, when you get those funny butterfly flutters in your tummy next time, you'll recognise them.'

Sarah laughed. 'It would take a darn sight more than a twinge of lust to convince me. If you want to play with Dr Dawson, you go right ahead. Just leave me out of it.'

'But he's expecting you to come on this visit to the village tomorrow. He was most insistent that I persuade you to come with us.'

'He'll get over it.'

'But what are you going to do while I'm gone?'

'Swim,' Sarah said decisively. 'A real swim, not just splashing around on the shoreline. I might head for one of the other islands. Some of them are only a kilometre or two away.'

'But what about sharks?'

'I'll try not to bleed in the water and attract them.'

Tori shuddered visibly. 'Rather you than me. I'd stay close enough to the shore to get to safety if I were you.'

'You're not me. That's the whole point. While you're away doing something you want to do, I can do things *I* want to do that don't interest you. It's perfect. We'll both enjoy ourselves. And we'll both survive, I promise.'

Tori turned, her face a picture of enlightenment. 'Ben is *your* shark,' she said. 'Isn't he?'

Sarah just smiled. 'Shall we have a quick swim in the dark before we go to bed?'

'You can't see sharks in the dark.'

'We'll stay very close to the shore.'

Tori giggled. 'And we won't bleed.'

'Definitely not.'

'OK. On one condition.'

'What's that?'

'If I'm prepared to risk my shark then you have to risk yours. The next time Ben asks you to spend some time with him, you have to say yes.'

'Not tomorrow. I really want a proper swim.'

'The time after that, then.'

'Sure.' It was a safe enough agreement. Sarah would bet Ben Dawson had more than enough experience to know where any pay-off was likely to be. After she refused to accompany them to the village tomorrow, he would get the message she wasn't interested and focus on Tori. And that way Sarah would be free to focus on enjoying every moment of the paradise she was discovering.

*   *   *

It just didn't get any better than this.

The sea was calm enough to be masquerading as the world's biggest swimming pool. Cool enough to be refreshing and allow the best physical workout Sarah had had in a long time. Treading water for a minute, Sarah shaded her eyes over the snorkelling mask she was wearing and took her bearings again to make sure she was still heading in the right direction.

It was just as well she had discussed her intentions with Nasoya, the man who looked after the diving equipment at the resort, when she had gone to borrow a mask and flippers. Her first choice of island was out of bounds, being the 'honeymoon' island. A tiny dot in the Pacific Ocean, it boasted an acre of palm forest and a single beach. Honeymooners could be dropped off, along with a luxury picnic, to spend the day in total privacy on an island of their own, and no one else could visit when it was being used.

So Sarah was heading for a larger island a little further away. This had a small village on it that supported itself growing sugar cane, and while Nasoya was impressed with Sarah's energy he was much happier knowing that there would be a boat available to bring her back if she changed her mind about swimming. He would let the village know she was coming, he told her, and she could have something to eat and drink there if she wished.

The invitation was becoming more attractive after the effort of nearly an hour's swimming. Sarah could see waves breaking near the entrance to the lagoon of the new island. There were fishing boats dotted sparsely nearby and Sarah could finally see the white strip of sand that marked her finishing point. A rest in the sun and maybe a fresh coconut with the top lopped off so she could drink the milk would be heaven.

The small, canoe-like boat with three children on board was on the sea side of the lagoon entrance and Sarah watched the boy in charge gauging which wave to catch to carry them through. He looked about nine or ten years old and seemed far too young for such a responsibility, but maybe island children grew up fast. There was another boy on board and a little girl who looked barely more than a toddler. Sarah trod water again briefly, looking over her shoulder as she wondered whether there was a parent in one of the nearby fishing boats, but they were all too far away to seem associated with the children.

The older boy chose a wave and paddled furiously to get ahead of it. The water surged behind the boat, lifting it up and pushing it forward. The small girl shrieked with delight as their speed increased but Sarah could feel her heart miss a beat. Sure enough, the boy's paddling wasn't strong enough to keep the boat in a straight line. It tipped sideways as the wave broke and to Sarah's horror the boat overturned and the three children vanished beneath a layer of white foam.

For several heartbeats she could see nothing. The wave was spent. The fishing boats were still bobbing at a distance. The island backdrop looked like paradise and the lagoon was still. And empty. Sarah could almost think she had imagined the whole scene. Then an object surfaced from the still water beyond the waves. A smooth object.

The hull of an overturned boat.

There was no time or breath to waste on exclamations of dismay. Sarah was swimming for all she was worth now. She needed to catch a wave at the right point herself so that she didn't end up on the dangerous coral reef that bordered the lagoon. Using the powerful overarm stroke that had won competitions in her school days, Sarah got ahead of the next wave forming and stayed with it as it carried her through the gap. The breaking surf pushed her below the surface for what seemed far too long and she shot up finally to catch her breath and start a frantic visual sweep of the calm water around her.

The older boy was still in the water, trying to help the younger one climb on top of the slippery boat hull. He was shouting and someone must have heard over the sound of the surf because more than one fishing boat was now heading in their direction. But where was the other child?

Sarah swam towards the boat. 'Where is she?' she called.

The boys both turned. Both looked frightened and neither answered her. Maybe they couldn't understand her. She took just another second to check that both these children were clinging onto the boat well enough to keep themselves safe and then she turned, desperately searching the surface of the lagoon for any sign of the small girl. She would be floating…unless she was drowning, in which case she would be under the water and not on top of it.

Sarah dived and swam using a rapid breaststroke. Thank goodness the water was so clear. She could see the colours of the coral bed, the startling shapes of sea anemones and the astonishing diversity of the swarms of fish. There were so many fish it made it difficult to see anything else, in fact. Forced to surface, Sarah dragged in a huge gulp of air and then used her flippers to push down and reach the depths of the lagoon again.

It was harder to hold her breath this time. Looking ahead as far as she could, Sarah swam doggedly forward, unaware of the extraordinary beauty of her surroundings, totally focussed on finding something she couldn't see. The burning in her lungs forced her upwards again and this time she had to take several painful gasps of air.

A fishing boat had reached the boys now and they were being pulled aboard. Another boat was riding the crest of a wave into the lagoon and Sarah could hear shouting from the shore. Islanders were gathering and some were running into the water. They would find the child with such numbers searching but it could well be too late by then. Sarah dragged in as much air as she could and went under the water again.

She didn't swim forward this time. She stayed in one spot and turned slowly, scanning a full three hundred and sixty degrees, concentrating on areas that were obscured by the tendrils of sea plants.

And there she was. The little girl was floating just above the coral, looking for all the world as though she was peacefully asleep except that her eyes were wide open. Sarah's heart lurched painfully enough to compete with the agony of lungs screaming for air but the surge of adrenaline was enough to propel her towards the small body. It was no real effort to take hold of the limp form and drag it towards the surface. Please, God, she cried silently, don't let me be too late.

It wasn't possible to do more than try a couple of breaths while she was in the water but somehow

Sarah summoned the energy to swim rapidly to shore, towing the child under one arm. The villagers fell silent as she ran through the shallows and they stepped back when she laid the girl on the damp sand, opened her airway and felt for a pulse. A woman wailed—a high keening sound that conveyed the very clear message that they knew it was too late.

But it wasn't. Sarah could feel a faint carotid pulse. She covered the girl's mouth and nose with her own and transferred a breath. And then another. Her fingers searched the small neck for a pulse again and were rewarded with a stronger beat. And then the limp form of the child twitched. A dark tangle of eyelashes fluttered and her mouth opened. Sarah turned her onto her side at the gagging sound she made and then held the little girl as her body convulsed, expelling the astonishing amount of water that had been swallowed, until the vomiting gave way to a distressed crying.

Sarah had never been happier to hear the sound of a miserable child. She rocked the girl in her arms, knowing that she had tears on her face and a stupidly wide grin as she looked up to find someone better able to give comfort.

There was more than comfort to be found. Both Sarah and the children were whisked back to the village to be fussed over in an atmosphere of having been part of a miracle. Once the small girl was wrapped in a blanket and happily asleep in her mother's arms, Sarah became the total focus of the islanders' attention. She could understand very little of what was being said but it was obvious she had made friends for life on this island.

An hour later, with wreaths of flowers crowding

her neck, a pile of gifts at her feet and an array of food and drink she couldn't possibly have coped with, Sarah was relieved to see a new arrival at the village. Somebody had contacted Nasoya, from the dive centre at the resort, and he had come with a boat to collect her. There was no way she could have managed the return swim, quite apart from the pile of gifts. The rescue had been physically exhausting and the emotional aftermath had left her simply wanting to curl up and sleep.

Nasoya wasn't the only arrival, however. Just behind him came two figures that Sarah had certainly not expected to see.

'News travels fast in these parts,' Ben told her. 'How does it feel to be a heroine?'

Sarah extracted herself from Tori's hug. 'Tiring.' She smiled. 'Can you check on little Milika? She seems OK but she came very close to drowning and she may well have some fluid in her lungs.'

'That's what I'm here for.' Ben held up the kit he was carrying. 'I just wanted to check that you were all right first.'

'I'm fine,' Sarah assured them both. 'All I need is a quiet spot in the sun to rest.'

A short time later the boat sped back to the resort island over a calm sea that gave no hint of the kind of horror it had engendered only a short time ago. Sarah sat quietly, still exhausted but very happy. Ben had examined Milika thoroughly and pronounced her none the worse for her ordeal.

'It was a dry drowning, thank goodness. First hint of cold water gave her laryngeal spasm. I doubt that even a drop got into her lungs. She must have swallowed a fair bit, though.'

'She did. I've never seen such a small child throw up such a large quantity of fluid.'

'All she needs now is a good rest. As you do.' Ben's glance had only been that of a concerned physician, so why did it feel like so much more? 'Are you sure you don't need a check-up?'

Sarah turned away, flushing with something rather more than embarrassment. 'I'm sure. I'll spend the afternoon resting and I'll be absolutely fine.'

When they arrived back at the resort's landing jetty, Tori helped to gather up the gifts, which included a traditional grass skirt.

'I can just see you in this,' she told Sarah. 'It's gorgeous.'

'You'll be able to wear it tonight,' Ben added.

Sarah turned at his confident tone. 'Why?'

'Didn't you hear all the planning going on around you? There's going to be a huge party to celebrate. There'll be two or three villages involved by the time all the friends and relatives get the news.'

'I can't go to something like that,' Sarah protested. 'It's *their* celebration.'

'They're doing it to honour you,' Ben said. His dark eyes caught and held Sarah's. 'You saved the life of a child, Sarah. They're doing this to thank you.'

'But—'

'They've already killed a pig,' Tori put in. She shuddered. 'I saw them choosing the fattest one they could find and then leading it away.'

'They'll roast the pig,' Ben said. 'But most of the food will be cooked in a traditional underground oven. A lovo. It's an experience not everyone gets.'

'But—'

'I'll come and collect you at seven o'clock.' Ben
was still holding Sarah's gaze.

'You're coming, too?' Suddenly, the invitation was
much less daunting.

'Of course.' Ben's smile looked almost smug. 'I've
been delegated to accompany you so, please, don't
embarrass me by refusing to come.'

Tori aimed a gentle kick at Sarah's ankle. 'Sharks,'
she murmured.

Ben looked nonplussed. 'You don't have to worry
about sharks,' he said. 'There'll be a lot of boats going over.' His grin was disarming. 'We don't expect
you to swim.'

'Am I invited?' Tori asked.

'Of course.' But Ben was still watching Sarah. 'It
won't be much of a party without a guest of honour,
though. How 'bout it, Sarah?'

'Were you serious? About me wearing the grass
skirt?'

'It's up to you. You're an honorary member of that
village for the rest of your life and they'll be dressed
up. They'd be very proud if you did wear it.'

Ben's gaze suggested *he* would be proud as well
and Sarah found herself nodding.

'OK, then. We'll see you at seven o'clock.'

'You're not really going to wear it, are you?' Tori
eyed the wrap-around skirt dubiously. 'It's awfully
see-through when you move.'

'I'll wear something underneath.' The deep sleep
Sarah had had for several hours that afternoon had
revived her completely. Now showered, with her hair
washed and gleaming softly as she brushed it dry in
the sun, she was ready for the new experience that

the evening promised to offer. Not only ready, she was going to embrace it completely. 'I'll wear it over that red skirt I've got.'

The mid-calf-length, soft muslin skirt was perfect. Cut in flared panels, it fitted closely around Sarah's hips and widened to drape in folds that did nothing to interfere with the fall of the dried grass of the island skirt she fastened on top. The flash of colour that showed when she moved was pleasing and Sarah chose a simple white halter-neck top to go with it.

'Sandals?' Tori was fishing around in the bottom of their wardrobe. 'Do you want the dressy ones or your flipflops?'

'I'm going barefoot,' Sarah told her.

'Cool. I will, too, then. Just as well we painted our toenails.'

Sarah pushed a headband into place to hold her hair back from her face. Then she tucked a large crimson flower to one side. The left side. She hung one of the many garlands she had been given that morning around her neck.

'You look like you were born here,' Tori exclaimed in delight. 'Especially with your hair loose like that. You should wear it down more often—it's gorgeous!'

'It's much easier to handle if it's tied up. I couldn't wear it loose at work.'

'You don't spend your whole life at work, you know.'

'I know. It just feels like it sometimes.' Sarah grinned as she did a twirl in front of the mirror. Her naturally olive skin had darkened to a rich brown with only a couple of days of the Fijian sun, and amazingly she did look almost like a child of the islands. 'This doesn't feel like me at all. It's dressing up. Part of the fantasy. And I intend to enjoy every minute of it.'

She had no choice but to enjoy herself. The look on Ben's face when he arrived to collect them made any effort to look as though she belonged more than worthwhile. He might be a practised flirt and utterly insincere but the admiration was still something that could be appreciated as part of this whole experience. Sarah was made to feel totally desirable with that one glance and it went to her head like a glass of champagne.

The cheer that went up from the islanders waiting in the fleet of small boats added more bubbles to this new effervescent sensation, and when they were gliding over early sunset-gilded waters towards the neighbouring island and a song broke out and spread between the boats, Sarah closed her eyes and sighed from the sheer pleasure of it all.

Just to have been an observer would have made it a magic night, but Sarah was at the centre of it all. She was carried into the village and given a place of honour on a flower-strewn mat where little Milika and her mother were waiting to sit beside her. Plied with the most delicious food, from spit-roasted pork, steamed fish and vegetables from the underground oven to fruit that needed no tampering with to provide the sweetest dessert, Sarah was entertained with song, dance and even fire-walking as villagers competed to put on the best show. Bowl after bowl of kava came her way and Sarah sipped at each one, hoping that they weren't alcoholic enough to cause regret in the morning.

The party showed no signs of letting up, even well

after Milika had fallen asleep in Sarah's lap and been carried away to her own bed. It was Sarah's turn to dance then, and there were any number of willing young men and women ready to teach her and Tori the movements. If Sarah felt a bit wobbly on her feet to start with, thanks to all the kava, the positive side was a lack of any inhibition. She could turn and stamp and sway her hips with the best of them, her arms tracing graceful arcs in the flickering firelight, her skirt and her curtain of shining dark hair swirling ever more joyously to the insistent beat of the drums.

It was at the height of the revelry when Sarah twirled a little too fast, or too many times in succession, lost her balance and then stumbled. Fortunately, she had been on the edge of the large group of people and a hibiscus bush screened her fall so it went unnoticed.

Almost unnoticed. The hands that reached to help her to her feet were Ben's, and when Sarah found herself pulled into his arms as she tried to regain her balance, she didn't protest. It was part of the fantasy of the night. Here she was, giddy from all the attention and the kava and the joy of the celebration—in the arms of admittedly the most gorgeous man she had ever met. And nobody could see them thanks to the screen of foliage, so it didn't matter that Sarah leaned into those arms just a little closer and raised her face to catch Ben's gaze.

But it wasn't his eyes that caught her attention first. It was his lips. Serious-looking, unsmiling lips.

Soft, inviting lips.

Was she willing them to come closer…to seek out her own? If so, it was working a treat and it was also so much part of the fantasy that Sarah didn't bother even questioning it. She closed her eyes and waited for their touch. Knowing that this would be the most exciting kiss she had ever received.

She wasn't disappointed. The caress was as soft as a butterfly's kiss to start with but the shock wave reverberated through every cell of her body. The shock was enough to make her gasp softly, parting her lips to do so, and because there was no air between her lips and Ben's, it was an invitation to explore further. An invitation that Ben didn't hesitate to accept.

She would never know how long that kiss lasted. Time ceased to exist. Nothing existed but the taste of Ben's mouth, the pressure of his lips and the exquisite slide of his tongue sending spirals of pleasure sharp enough to seem like pain coursing through her body. The background harmony of voices raised in song faded but the beat of the drums matched that of Sarah's heart and only fed the sensation of utter bliss.

Ben's arms tightened around her and Sarah could feel the whole hard length of his body pressed against hers. This was crazy. One kiss, and Sarah was ready to abandon any rules she had about men. Ready to step over a brink she had never crossed before—to hurl herself headlong into a pleasure she had never believed actually existed. She couldn't stop and it didn't matter because she couldn't conceive of *wanting* to stop.

It was just as well that Ben could. He pulled away and the time that had passed couldn't have been an eternity because they were still alone and unnoticed. He didn't let her go immediately, however. Sarah felt his arms still tight around her.

'Well, I never,' Ben murmured. 'You do have

something special you like to keep hidden, don't you, Sarah?'

The jolt back to reality was harsh. Had Ben kissed her to check out whether she was really as 'uptight' as he had supposed?

Sarah pulled away from his arms. 'Oh, my God,' she whispered. 'That should *not* have happened.'

'Why not?' Ben sounded amused.

'What's Tori going to think?'

'I'm sure she'd think it was all part of the fun.'

'She would, if it was *her* that you were kissing.' Sarah shook her head, stepping back and smoothing the ruffled grass of her skirt. 'I just hope she didn't see that.'

'It really doesn't have anything to do with her, does it?' Ben was watching Sarah as she pushed stray tresses of hair behind her shoulders. He was still close enough to be heard easily over the sounds of the party continuing behind them and he looked puzzled. 'I think *I'm* allowed to choose whom I want to kiss, aren't I?'

Sarah felt a little confused herself. 'But Tori likes you.'

'Don't you like me, Sarah?' Ben's voice was teasing. As soft and seductive as his lips had been only seconds ago. He was pulling her back, turning her convictions upside down, making her want things she had never thought she could want this much.

'No...not like that.' Sarah needed to escape. To get to shore and get away from any possible nibbles from a shark. Any *more* nibbles, anyway. 'Tori's my sister, or as good as. She's also my best friend. I'm not going to poach a man she's interested in.'

'But I'm not interested in Tori,' Ben said. 'I'm not

interested in any woman, for that matter. Not seriously, anyway.' He was clearly withdrawing. Scared off maybe? A branch of hibiscus was being held back so that Sarah could rejoin the party. 'If it's not fun, it's not worth bothering with,' he said tersely. 'Let's forget it, shall we?'

'Good idea.' Sarah straightened her back and walked past Ben. The statement had summed him up perfectly and Sarah knew her initial impression of the man had been the genuine one. Disappointment that could easily become anger was chasing away the confusion that kiss had caused. Ben Dawson was dangerous. He couldn't give a damn how other people felt or whether they would be hurt by his actions. He couldn't be part of any fun as far as Sarah was concerned, and for that purpose she would have to agree with him. He wasn't worth bothering with.

She would just have to make sure Tori realised that as well.

CHAPTER THREE

How could she have been so gullible?

Tori had agreed readily, as they had finally prepared for bed last night, that Ben Dawson was a lowlife, ready to take advantage of any woman stupid enough to fall for his surface charm. The resigned twist of her face had suggested that the revelation was only to be expected, and she had sighed, indicating that she may have surrendered any notion of being one of those women.

'Well, at least *you* kissed him, Sas.'

Sarah's brush had caught on a tangle somewhere in the length of her hair. Had the knot been caused by Ben's fingers as they had burrowed for a better grip on her head in order to angle her lips to meet his? She'd welcomed the pain of forcing the bristles through the obstruction.

'I wish I hadn't.'

'Why?' Tori had pulled up the sheet on her bed to cover her bare shoulders. 'Was he no good?'

Sarah snorted. 'I wouldn't say that exactly.' She'd known she would never forget that kiss. She'd had a horrible feeling she would never experience anything that had the chance of competing with it again, and *that* was why she wished it had never happened. But how could he not have been good…with the amount of practice he'd had?

'Hmm.'

* * *

That murmur of agreement took on a whole new tone in hindsight as Sarah balanced the paddle on her canoe and watched Tori glide further ahead. It had been an interested 'hmm', not one of agreement. All she had done had been to fuel Tori's curiosity, hadn't she? And in her usual determined style, her foster-sister had gone right ahead planning her next move, cunningly avoiding telling Sarah because she knew jolly well she shouldn't be doing it.

'I'm not going to do this, Tori,' she called. 'It's a bad idea. I don't want any part of it.'

'OK.' Tori was still paddling. 'I'll go by myself.'

She would, too. How many times had she got Sarah into trouble by pulling exactly this kind of stunt? The first time had been only a week after Sarah had moved in with the Prestons. Tori had wanted to play in the 'out of bounds' area of bush near the house and had tearfully convinced Sarah that she'd lost her favourite toy there the week before. And Sarah had taken the flak for the small adventure because eight-year-old Tori had already managed to creep past the barrier around her heart with her ready acceptance of her new 'big sister' and the stream of small gifts and notes that had been under her pillow every night.

But this was a completely different ball game. It wasn't an adventure in a dangerous forest that Tori wanted.

Tori wanted to play with Ben Dawson.

Sarah should have been suspicious when, despite her fear of sharks in the open sea, it had been Tori's idea to hire canoes and explore one of the uninhabited islands nearby. She should have been even more suspicious when Tori had spent rather a long time with the young Fijian, Jolame, in charge of the canoes.

He'd seemed only too happy to talk, laugh and point out which islands were suitable destinations while Sarah had been choosing their canoes and paddles.

Sarah had remained innocent of Tori's real agenda for just a little too long. She had been too preoccupied by her enjoyment of the physical activity, following Tori's lead as she'd dipped her paddle and pulled against the resistance of the water. One side, then the other—falling into an easy rhythm that allowed her to appreciate the splash of droplets catching the light and glistening like diamonds, and the irresistible allure of the tiny islands adorning the blue expanse of the Pacific Ocean around them.

Finally, the unusually hilly outline of the island they were heading towards registered.

'We can't go to that island,' she exclaimed. 'It's privately owned.'

'Is it?' Tori didn't seem convincingly surprised. Or perturbed that an hour's paddling time might have been misdirected.

'Can't you see that house? You can't just turn up on someone's private island.'

'We'll go round the other side.'

'I was told specifically not to land on any privately owned islands when I went for that swim yesterday. Look...' Sarah waved her arm in a wide circle. 'There's a dozen islands around here and most of them are closer to ours. Why have you made a beeline for *this* one?'

Tori said nothing.

'Oh, *no*!' Sarah groaned. 'Who owns this island, Tori?'

'I have no idea.'

'*Victoria!*'

'OK, OK. Yes, I *think* it's Ben's island. He's having a day off today so maybe he'll be at home.'

'If he'd wanted visitors he would have issued an invitation.'

'Maybe it will be a nice surprise.'

'No. We're not doing this.'

'*I* am.' Tori's canoe was already pulling ahead as Sarah stowed her paddle across the top of hers. 'Look, he won't know it was deliberate. There's no house on the other side of the island and there's a nice little beach. If we happen to go for a walk and meet him, well…it'll just be a happy coincidence, won't it? Stop worrying, Sas. It's no big deal.'

Sarah had to paddle hard to catch up with Tori again. It *was* a big deal and it had the potential to get a lot bigger if she left Tori to her own devices. It wasn't hard to see that Tori was tiring from the physical effort she'd already expended in reaching her goal. Maybe Sarah could salvage the situation even if they were caught trespassing by explaining that they'd lost their sense of direction and Tori had needed a rest to be sure of getting back to the resort safely.

'We'll land on the beach, then,' she conceded. 'Have the picnic they gave us, a swim and a rest, and then we're heading home. We are *not* going to go walking off to see if we can surprise Dr Dawson.'

'OK.' Tori appeared to be far more concerned about something else now. 'Oh, my God! Was that a fin?'

'I can't see anything.'

'Those waves look huge. What if I tip sideways and there *is* a shark?'

'Hold that thought.' Sarah had to smile at Tori's expression. 'Let's turn around and go home.'

'Oh, no, you don't!' With a renewed burst of determination, Tori turned and paddled towards the breaking surf. The waves weren't actually very big at all and Tori was so pleased with herself at successfully negotiating the ride she didn't wait until the canoe reached the shore to stand up. Sarah saw the paddle do a graceful arc as Tori fell backwards into shallow water, whereupon it got sucked back with a receding wave. When the abandoned canoe showed signs of following, Sarah dived into the water to catch hold of it.

'Oops.' Tori was wading out to help with the struggle and they dragged both canoes up onto the beach. 'Did you get my paddle?' She bit her lip at Sarah's expression. 'Oops, again.' Her smile was nowhere near contrite, however. 'Just as well the picnic is in *your* canoe, huh?'

They sat on the sand in the shade of an ancient palm tree. The beach was a delight. The small cove they were in appeared to be cut off from the rest of the island by steeply sloping sides created by a tumble of dark volcanic rock. The shrubbery below the palms was dense and they would be invisible unless someone actually set foot on the beach. Sarah relaxed just a little. The deed had been done and it *was* an irresistibly beautiful spot, so they may as well enjoy it for a short time. Tori misinterpreted her sigh of contentment as Sarah reached for the contents of the picnic basket.

'Maybe the paddle will get washed back in.'

'Doubt it. I'll have to tow you back. We should be able to find a length of vine that could act as a rope.'

'We could always go and see if Ben has a spare paddle somewhere.'

'No, we couldn't.'

Tori was silent until they had eaten their fill of the fresh sandwiches and fruit they had been provided with. Then she wriggled into the sun, stripped off her T-shirt and reached for the bottle of sunscreen.

'I'm going to be *so* brown when we get home. Everyone's going to know I've been on a tropical island holiday.' She lay back and closed her eyes. 'Are you going to swim?'

'I'll let my lunch go down a bit first.' The meal on top of the physical exertion and the heat was making Sarah feel decidedly drowsy. She stayed in the shade but followed Tori's example and curled up on the sand, rolling her towel into a pillow. 'Don't get too much sun. You burn more easily than I do, remember.'

'I'll be careful.' Tori rolled over onto her stomach. 'Mind you, if I got sunburnt, I'd have to call for a doctor, wouldn't I?'

Sarah made an exasperated sound and closed her eyes. Tori took the hint and lapsed into silence so that the only sound was the gentle and rhythmic breaking of the waves.

She had had no intention of falling asleep and she had absolutely no idea how long she had been asleep for, but something had alerted a sixth sense and Sarah's eyes opened smartly. Sure enough, she was alone on the beach.

A moment's panic at the thought that Tori might have gone swimming alone was easily dismissed. Tori would never swim in the open sea without someone on watch for sharks. That left a land-based destination that had attracted her, and Sarah's sinking heart told her exactly what that was.

Leaping to her feet, Sarah scanned the beach, following the line of footprints in the soft sand. Waves broke with far more ferocity on the wall of black rock that marked the end of the beach. Surely Tori wouldn't have attempted negotiating such a dangerous route?

No. The track Sarah was now following led towards the back of the small cove where a tiny waterfall had remained hidden by trees and rocks. The beauty of the small, clear pool it formed at its base before the rock gave way to pure white sand barely registered, and Sarah also failed to hear the musical splash of the water or notice the scent of the exotic wild flowers half-hidden by ferns.

Her attention was focussed on higher ground and the safest way to reach it. Tough, springy grass grew between the rocks as the ground levelled out further up and it looked almost like a track before fading under the shade of more trees. The rock formation was rough enough to provide easy steps and handholds.

'Tori!'

Sarah paused on the top of the rocks, scanning the beach once more before it disappeared from view. The bright blue of their canoes made a splash of very obvious colour even against the glare of the white sand. The red of Tori's bikini would have been just as easy to spot.

'Tori!'

Sarah's call was much louder this time. The worry that had led her gaze reluctantly out to sea, half ex-

pecting the horror of seeing a flash of red drifting with
the tide, morphed into anger.

How could Tori have been stupid enough to take
off by herself like this? There could be wild pigs on
this island. Or poisonous spiders. Did Fiji have
snakes? Sandals were hardly appropriate footwear to
be rock-climbing in. The smooth patches on these
rocks looked invitingly easy to cross but they were
slippery under flat rubber soles and if you were in a
hurry because you were doing something you knew
you *shouldn't* be doing, it would be only too easy to
slip.

Sarah shuddered inwardly as she glanced to one
side at the remains of the ancient volcano that flowed
right into the sea. She was at a height of several metres above sea level now, and it was only too easy to
imagine how unforgiving that black rock would be if
she fell.

The glance was so quick, Sarah had turned to take
another step before she realised what her peripheral
vision had caught. As her head jerked back she had
dismissed the notion as a product of an overactive
imagination but was compelled to double-check.

'Tori!' There was no anger in her call this time. It
was pure horror. She hadn't imagined the flash of red,
and now, looking down, she could see the pale shape
of limbs in the shadow of an overhanging rock. Limbs
that weren't moving and were far too close to the
reach of breaking waves.

Sarah welcomed the feeling of calm detachment
that allowed her to cope so well with emergencies in
her job. Personal fear and anguish were jammed into
a compartment that Sarah was very good at keeping
locked. She could assess the situation, plan what

needed to be done and then take the logical steps to make sure that happened as quickly as possible.

Backtracking and climbing over the rocks at sea level would take too long. There was no safe way straight down but Sarah could see a route further ahead. She slid down a short, grassy bank and then climbed carefully down a series of huge boulders before scrambling up over another series to reach Tori.

For a moment anguish surfaced, and it was Tori's face Sarah reached to touch instead of checking her airway. When Tori's eyes opened at her touch, Sarah had to swallow a painful lump in her throat and the threat of tears of relief.

'Sas!' Tori actually managed a smile. 'I've really done it this time, haven't I?'

'You're an idiot,' Sarah agreed, but her answering smile was decidedly wobbly. 'What hurts?'

'My leg, mostly.'

Sarah pulled her gaze away from Tori's face. A moment later, she groaned aloud. 'You've broken it,' she told Tori. 'Tib and fib at midshaft.'

'I thought so.' Tori closed her eyes again. 'How bad is it?'

'Bad enough.' Sarah was pulling off the sarong she had knotted at her waist. It was far from sterile but any cover over such a nasty, open wound with broken bones exposed was better than nothing. A desperate glance around them showed nothing that could potentially provide a splint, not even a stick of driftwood.

The touch of water lapping at her feet as Sarah moved added to her fears. She was going to have to move Tori very soon.

'Did you hit your head? Were you knocked out?'

'No, I don't think so. I remember hearing my leg

break. My shoulder hurts a bit, too, and I might have dented a few ribs.'

'Are you having any trouble breathing?'

'No. It's just a bit sore if I take a deep breath.'

'How's your neck?'

Tori turned her head slowly from side to side. 'It's fine. I can still wiggle everything except I'm not sure about the toes on my right foot. Are they moving?'

'No.' Sarah bit her lip. With neurological compromise like that from the fracture, it was urgent to straighten and splint Tori's lower leg. 'I'm going to have to go for help,' she decided aloud.

'Sorry.' Tori opened her eyes again. 'I really am, Sas. I didn't mean this to happen.'

'Of course you didn't.' Sarah was watching a new wave breaking. 'Trouble is, the tide's coming in and I don't know how long it will take me to get help so I'm going to have to move you a bit further up.' She looked over her shoulder. 'I could climb up and try and find something to splint your leg with first.'

'No. That'll take too long.' With an obviously painful effort Tori pushed herself up onto one elbow. 'I can help. You drag me and I'll push with my good foot. Do we need to go far?'

'If we can get you on top of this flatter rock it should be enough. If you can stand on your good leg, I can turn you and then lift your legs.'

It worked. Just. Tori was as white as a sheet by the time she was upright, sweating and nauseated as she was turned, and she almost passed out from the pain as Sarah supported her legs and lifted them. With impressive determination, however, she managed to drag herself back until her back was supported by another rock.

'I'm going to be sick.'

'Might be better if you lie flat.'

'No. I want to keep an eye on those waves. I might need to move again before you get back.'

'I hope not. I'll be as quick as I can.'

'I know.' Tori's lip trembled and she gave up any attempt to smile. 'You'd better get going, Sas. Don't worry. I'll be all right.'

The total area of Ben Dawson's private island was probably less than five acres, but without knowing how untamed the areas of vegetation were it would be taking too big a risk to try and cross the island on foot.

Sarah retraced her steps, ran across the burning sand of the cove and dragged her canoe back into the waves. She paddled harder than she had imagined she was capable of, ignoring the discomfort of muscle fatigue, shortness of breath and the sweat that made her look as if she'd been under rather than on top of the water. Within minutes she rounded the outcrop of rocks that marked the other end of the cove from where Tori was lying and she could see the sliver of white sand advertising the long beach near the dwelling they had spotted.

Any thought that invading Ben's privacy on his day off would be less than welcome had been overtaken by an overwhelming hope that this *was* indeed his island and that he *would* be at home on his day off. Tori needed help, fast, and if that help was medically qualified with equipment to back it up, it would be a huge bonus.

This beach was much larger than the cove on the other side of the island. A jet boat was moored to a jetty and a well-marked path curved beneath palm trees towards a traditional-looking bure with a thatched roof and sides. As Sarah was forced to slow down and catch her breath, she realised that the bure was not so traditional. Tall louvred windows were set into solid-looking framing along a stretch of veranda furnished with very comfortable-looking wicker furniture. A satellite dish was only partly disguised by the thatching of the roof and the hum of a powerful generator could be heard coming from a small thatched hut she passed.

That hum was the only sound, however. The front entrance to the house stood open but there was nobody in sight. Sarah paused, uncertain, before climbing the steps to the veranda.

'Hello! Is anybody home?'

A sound more distant than the noise of the generator made her turn. From somewhere behind a garden that boasted the most extraordinary orchids she had ever seen, a slow, rhythmic knocking was now going on. Hammering, perhaps?

Then the sound of a door clicking shut made her swing back towards the house. She ran up the steps and banged on the wood.

'Hello!' she shouted. 'Help! I need help!'

There was no response. Had the door closed of its own accord somehow? But then Sarah heard another door closing somewhere within the house and she had the distinct impression that any further calling would be of no avail. She wasn't welcome here and whoever was in the house was going to pretend there was no one home.

Should she try the doorhandle? Go inside if it hadn't been locked and confront whoever might be in residence? But what if it wasn't Ben? She'd be wasting precious time if she found someone who didn't speak her own language. She did have another option, didn't she? The deliberation took only a split second and then Sarah was running again, this time in the direction of the hammering sound.

The trunk of the old banana tree was surprisingly resistant to the blows of even a freshly sharpened axe, but strenuous physical effort was exactly what the doctor had ordered as far as Ben Dawson was concerned. The sharp discomfort of each impact as it reverberated up his right arm and lodged somewhere under his shoulder blade was not nearly enough to make him want to stop.

Chop!

Why had he given in to the temptation of kissing Sarah Mitchell last night? Why had he even broken his own rule of not leaving home after reasonable working hours unless it was a medical emergency?

Chop!

Because something had drawn him inexorably towards Sarah from the moment he'd seen her sitting on the beach with that book. The attention of her bubbly foster-sister had been welcome only because it had provided an excuse to be near her again. The disappointment when she had taken off to go swimming instead of coming to the village yesterday had been astonishingly sharp, but then fate had thrown another opportunity his way when she'd saved that child from drowning.

Chop!

Ben could feel the knot in his shoulder tighten a notch and sweat trickled from his hairline and stung painfully as it reached his eyes. What had possessed him to suggest that Sarah wear the grass skirt she'd been given? And how had she managed to transform herself into a form that could have stepped from one of the fantasies he indulged in so rarely?

Velvety, olive skin on long graceful limbs. That gorgeous fall of silky, dark hair. Equally dark eyes that hinted at secrets she didn't choose to share. Maybe that was what had been so attractive about Sarah. Compelling, even. For some bizarre reason, Ben wanted very much to know what those secrets were. He might have even been prepared to share a few of his own.

Chop!

Pain forced him to rest the axe for a moment. Ben reached for the shirt lying amongst the ginger plants and mopped dirt and sweat from his face and bare chest. He should go inside. Mara would have lunch ready and Phoebe would be awake again soon. But the dead tree was almost felled, thank goodness, and as a bonus, any obsession with Sarah Mitchell was being concurrently chopped away.

As if he would have shared his secrets! And what point was there in getting involved with a woman who wouldn't be here next week? It was part of the attraction of living here, even on a temporary basis. It was so easy to avoid any real interest in any woman. A short fling here and there was fine, if somewhat embarrassing when they came looking for a repeat performance like that sunburnt one—Lisa. She understood the rules, though. They all did. A bit of fun. Nothing serious.

It was a game Sarah clearly had no desire to play and Ben had known the instant he'd seen her that she would consider the rules nothing more than a selfish justification of unacceptable behaviour. That should have put him off quicker than a rat up a drainpipe. It certainly shouldn't have started nibbling at his conscience. He'd got over his own disquiet concerning the moral implications long ago. It was the way things were here. Nobody got hurt because nobody wanted more than he was prepared to offer.

He screwed his damp, grimy shirt into a tight ball and flung it back into the shrubbery. What he had to offer wasn't good enough for Sarah, though, was it? She was quite prepared to hand him on to Tori as though he were a toy she had no interest in playing with.

But she *was* interested. Nobody could respond to a kiss like that if they weren't. In fact, even the most interested partners Ben had ever scored had never responded like that. It was the kiss that bothered him more than anything now. More than the way Sarah had backed off at the speed of light and told him it was Tori he should have been kissing. He couldn't forget the feel of her in his arms, the way she had melted against his body…the way she had tasted…

Dammit!

The final blow with the axe was forceful enough to complete the job. The tree teetered and then tipped sideways. Ben watched it fall, and at the precise moment it hit the ground with a jarring thud, he saw her.

He was dreaming. He had to be!

Sarah was wearing nothing but a white bikini bottom and a tiny singlet top that clung to her skin as though she had just stepped from the waves. Maybe she had. Maybe she had swum all the way here just to be with *him*. Ben closed his eyes and ran his hand

across his brow but she was still there when he
checked.

Her hair was braided again but it was coming loose,
with loops and tendrils hanging around her face. In
fact, Sarah looked like a wild creature. Dishevelled.
She was clearly trying to catch her breath and she
looked more than a little frightened.

Of him? Ben's amazement faded as he realised he
probably looked just as wild as Sarah. He was half-
naked, hot and filthy—staring at her as if she were
some kind of apparition, with his hands gripping a
rather large axe.

Dropping the potential weapon, he smiled.
'Thought the heat had got to me for a moment there.
To what do I owe this pleasure?'

Sarah gulped in more air. 'Thank God…I found
you,' she managed. 'It's Tori—she needs you, Ben.'

Any building excitement was felled as cleanly as
that banana tree and Ben's smile faded just as rapidly.
Sarah hadn't come to see him for herself. She was
still trying to push him towards Tori.

'Oh?' His tone was cool. He could have forgiven
Sarah for breaking the rules and inviting herself here,
but this was unacceptable.

'She's hurt. Badly…'

He could see the fear in those dark eyes but it was
the wobble in her voice that undid him. He had become immune to women's tears in the last few years
but he knew Sarah would be an exception. He
couldn't let her cry. It would be a far more dangerous
form of trespassing than having her on his own turf.

'Tell me what's happened.' A professional query.
Assuming a degree of responsibility that was often
just what an anxious family needed in an emergency.

'She's fallen on rocks.' Sarah blinked hard, rallying, then hauled in a breath and spoke as fast as she could before she needed another one. 'She's got a compound fracture of her tib and fib. She may have rib and shoulder injuries, too. I've got her away from the water line but I don't know how far the tide comes in and—'

'Where is she?' Ben was close to Sarah now, close enough to touch her, but he managed to resist.

'We were on a little beach on the other side of this island.'

'Right. Let's go.' Ben was moving fast. 'I've got my kit in the boat. You get aboard.' He peeled off the path in the direction of the house. 'I'm just going to grab my phone in case we need extra help.'

Sarah couldn't help looking over her shoulder as that front door opened. Sure enough, she caught a glimpse of a shadowy figure inside and formed the distinct impression that the person was female, but she had no more than seconds to ponder the mystery before she heard Ben running behind her. He got to the boat before she did and held out a hand to help her jump into the vessel.

The grip was firm and as reassuring as the demand for information about Tori had been. It didn't matter that she had interrupted his day or trespassed on private property. Ben was going to help. To take charge. Sarah clung to the ray of hope that they would get through this ordeal as tightly as she clung to Ben's hand.

Maybe she held that hand for a second longer than she should have. The tight knot of fear in her stomach was suddenly split by a shaft of a very different sen-

sation—a twinge of lust that Tori would probably
have applauded but which made Sarah cringe. How
inappropriate was that? It had to be some kind of
reaction to her frantic worry about Tori and the very
real relief that she had found Ben.

Sarah watched the jetty grow smaller over the
foaming wake of the boat for several seconds before
stealing another glance at its pilot. How could she still
find him attractive when it was a completely different
person she was seeing than the man who had kissed
her last night?

That laid-back charm and easy smile had still been
there, albeit hidden behind his surprise and the grime
of physical labour, but it had been flicked off like a
light switch as soon as Sarah had started speaking.
Tension had taken its place. And authority. And a
professionalism that Sarah had to appreciate because
it was directed to helping Tori.

Strangely, the fact that Ben was still half-naked did
nothing to help resurrect the lightweight, playboy im-
age and maybe that was the reason for her bizarre
twinge. A serious, focussed Dr Dawson was a far
more attractive proposition. Not that she was about to
let him know that, of course, so when he turned his
head so swiftly she had no time to look away, Sarah
was caught off guard.

'How did you know where to find me?'

'I followed the noise of your hammering. Chopping,
I mean. Nobody answered the door at the house.' Any
impulse to ask why evaporated as Ben's face set into
grim lines.

'You said you'd ''found'' me. That implies you
were *looking* for me.'

'I…ah…' Sarah tried to marshal her thoughts. 'I *hoped* you might be here.'

'How did you get to this island anyway?'

'Canoe. I left mine on your beach. Didn't you see it?'

'No.'

Sarah had to hold onto the rail as the boat turned sharply to speed around the curve of the island.

'They must have told you which islands you could go to. I'm sure they would have told you this one was private.'

Sarah shook her head. They hadn't told *her*, had they? 'I'm sorry if we were trespassing,' she offered. 'But there are a lot of islands.'

'This one is very distinctive due to its height.' Ben was cutting back the throttle now and pointing them towards the shore. 'And I don't actually believe it was coincidence that you're here.'

The gaze that raked Sarah from head to foot was dismissive and it was only then that she remembered where her sarong was. Her singlet top covered her only to her belly button. Below that was just her bikini bottom and a long length of bare legs. That Ben thought she had shared Tori's motives and was throwing herself at him was humiliating. With her cheeks burning, Sarah leaped from the boat as soon as the hull scraped on sand. She helped Ben drag it further onto the beach and then she took off, stooping to gather both her towel and Tori's from beneath the palm tree before heading towards the end of the cove.

If Tori was in shock she would need something to cover her. How long had they been? Sarah had a very real fear that Tori could be unconscious from blood loss due to an undiagnosed internal injury or that her ribs could have punctured a lung and she was now unable to breathe, but fortunately those fears could be dismissed the instant she climbed onto that rock ledge.

Tori looked pale and miserable but she was conscious and breathing quite well enough to talk.

'Hey, you made it! Did you find Ben? Oh...' Tori spotted the figure behind Sarah. 'You *did* find him.'

'Funnily enough, she seemed to know where to look.' Ben had his fingers on Tori's wrist, feeling her pulse. 'How did this happen?'

'I was going for a walk. I slipped on those rocks.'

'What hurts the most?'

'My leg.'

Ben took the pad of fabric covering the wound off and whistled silently. 'You made a good job of that, didn't you? Sarah, could you get a dressing out of my kit, please? You'll find a splint and some bandages in there as well.' He had his fingers on the top of Tori's foot now, feeling for a pedal pulse. 'Can you wiggle your toes?'

'No.'

'Any paresthesia?'

'Yes. My whole foot feels kind of numb.'

'We're going to need to straighten it, then.' Ben glanced up to catch Tori's frightened expression and his face softened for the first time since Sarah had found him and told him of the emergency. 'Don't worry. I've got some morphine in that kit. Are you allergic to any drugs that you know of?'

'No.'

'Good. We'll start sorting this out, then, shall we?' Ben stood up and flipped open his phone. 'I'm just going to organise another boat and some help getting you off this rock. I'll let the hospital know you're coming. With a bit of luck they'll have a theatre available quickly. When did you last eat?'

'What?' Tori looked very close to tears now. 'I can't get *operated* on.'

'You've got an open fracture that looks highly likely to be complicated. It'll have to be cleaned out properly under general anaesthetic even if it doesn't need internal fixation.'

'*No!*'

'What do you mean, "no"?'

Sarah reached out to comfort Tori with her touch. 'I think the prospect of surgery in a place like Fiji is a bit of a worry.'

'I can assure you that the hospitals are not primitive. Fiji even has a medical school, you know.'

'You said yourself that this is likely to be a complicated fracture. We're hardly likely to find the kind of orthopaedic expertise we have at home, are we?'

Ben opened his mouth and then closed it again as though giving up any notion of challenging Sarah's assumptions.

'There's the question of a hospital stay as well,' Sarah added. 'And physiotherapy facilities. How soon would she be able to travel? Do we have any other options? We do have good medical insurance cover.'

'You could try for an emergency evacuation.' Ben's tone was brisk. 'The fracture could probably be reduced enough to prevent neurological deterioration without surgery, but that's going to depend on how soon a commercial or military flight is able to take you back to New Zealand. Is that what you would prefer?'

Sarah looked at Tori's frightened face and then met Ben's gaze calmly. 'If that's possible, yes.'

'Fine.' Ben's nod ended the discussion. 'We'll see what we can arrange.'

The tears in Tori's eyes finally overflowed. 'But what about our holiday?'

Ben's snort was not without sympathy as he turned towards his kit. 'I'd say the holiday is pretty much over, wouldn't you?'

CHAPTER FOUR

No DOUBT about it.

The holiday was over. Paradise had turned into something approaching hell and Sarah was left vowing she would never let Tori talk her into anything *ever* again.

It was all so awful, Sarah couldn't decide what the worst bit of it all actually was. Her lack of decision had nothing to do with the amount of consideration she gave it, because she'd had plenty of time to sit and wait and it was impossible to think of anything else.

Tori was injured and that was horrible, but it wasn't life-threatening and she would probably bounce back in time with nothing but a small scar as a memento. She had been miserable and in severe pain but Ben's treatment on scene had dealt with that effectively.

Rather too effectively.

With an IV cannula deftly inserted in Tori's arm and fluids running from the bag Sarah had been delegated to hold, Ben had given Tori a dose of morphine that had done more than eradicate her pain. Anyone would have thought she'd put away an unwise amount of pure alcohol!

'This wasn't meant to happen, y'know,' she'd confided to Ben as he'd splinted her leg.

'I'm sure it wasn't.'

'It was *my* idea.'

'Really?'

'Not to break my leg, silly! To come and find you!'

'Oh?' Ben's cool tone should have been enough of a warning but Tori's drug-induced euphoria made her oblivious and Sarah, in her position as bag-holder, was powerless to intervene.

'Well, Sarah doesn't want you, but I thought you were too cute to waste and she *said* you were a good kisser.'

The look Sarah had received had been humiliating to say the least. A brief, harsh glance but it had said it all. She had kissed and told. Not only that, she had kissed, told and had probably informed Tori that she wasn't interested so Ben was up for grabs.

If today's little adventure hadn't been her idea, he evidently thought she had at least encouraged Tori. Her complicity was undeniable given that they had both hired canoes, located their target and made a not inconsiderable effort to get here.

That look had to be the worst aspect of this whole, ghastly, long afternoon. Maybe if Ben had looked at her again, Sarah would have been able to put that glance into perspective, but he had managed to avoid any eye contact ever since. Or had Sarah been the one to keep her head down and focus on getting through the rest of this ordeal with minimum scarring?

It hadn't been too difficult after the rescue boat arrived, in any case. They had all been focussed on Tori, making sure her leg had been securely splinted, manoeuvring the stretcher over the rocks and then getting her into the larger boat waiting a little off-shore.

The fast trip to the main Fijian island of Viti Levu had Sarah's hair whipped into total disarray and the sarong she now had wrapped around her legs again did little to prevent her feeling chilled.

Excluded from the emergency department of Suva hospital, Sarah was left with an uncomfortably hard seat, noise and bustle and an avalanche of curious stares from a crowded waiting area. She saw Tori briefly as she was taken away for an X-ray and a temporary cast and then a nurse came to inform her that all necessary arrangements had been made.

'There's an army plane leaving from the airport in two hours' time.' The pretty Fijian Indian nurse spoke perfect English. 'They have space to evacuate Victoria, and they're happy for you to accompany your sister.'

'Will I have time to get back to the resort and collect our belongings?'

'That's been taken care of as well. They've been packed and should arrive here shortly.'

'Oh?' Sarah was taken aback. Any control of this situation had clearly been firmly removed from her own hands. 'Thanks… Who organised that?'

'Dr Dawson.'

Of course. He couldn't wait to pack them both up and ship them out, could he? No wonder, with Tori letting him know he rated only as a holiday plaything. But wasn't that initially how he'd wanted to come across? What gave him the right to be so judgmental now? Confusion, a curious disappointment and downright humiliation still lingering from *that* look warred with Sarah's anxiety about Tori and the embarrassment of causing inconvenience to a great many people.

Not that Nasoya, from their resort, seemed to mind.

'I need to shop,' he informed Sarah with a wide grin. 'I was coming to Suva anyway.'

He pulled the last bag from the wheelchair he was using as a luggage trolley. The zip on the large sports bag had not been fastened due to its bulging contents, and Sarah's embarrassment zoomed skywards as items tumbled to the worn linoleum of the waiting-room floor.

The cowrie shell Sarah had been given by little Milika bounced and then rolled rapidly to disappear beneath a curtain, but Sarah was too busy snatching up items of underwear to chase it.

'You bought too much.' Nasoya grinned, helpfully picking up one of Tori's lime-green bras. 'It didn't fit.'

Sarah's smile was tight, her cheeks aflame, and she didn't bother correcting the assumption. The extra luggage mostly comprised the gifts. Relief that most of the space in the soft carryall was taken up by the grass skirt chased away her embarrassment. It would have been very upsetting to lose that reminder of a very memorable occasion.

Sarah wanted that shell, too.

Ignoring the fact that she was providing entertainment to a large number of people, Sarah moved towards the curtained area and hesitated only briefly before poking her head through the gap. Maybe it was an overflow space from the main emergency department. It looked as though it could be used for a patient as it contained a bed…and a patient!

'Hello!'

'Hi.' The small girl sounded shy and didn't look up but she clearly spoke English and Sarah smiled.

'You haven't seen a shell that rolled under the curtain, have you?'

The girl nodded and turned as she held up the shell, and it was all Sarah could do not to gasp aloud.

It was as though she was seeing two different children. The profile she had seen initially was that of a pretty girl about four years old, with almost navy blue eyes and soft-looking blonde curls that reached her shoulders.

The other half of her face was a travesty of that prettiness. Boiled red, puckered skin pulled one eye, an ear and a corner of her mouth into misshapen lines and only tiny wisps of hair covered her temple on that side.

Such severe scarring could only have been caused by burns and Sarah's heart skipped a beat as she saw similar scarring down the length of the small arm holding up the shell.

Her own current ordeal ceased to be of any importance and Sarah had to control the urge to gather this child into her arms. Instead, she crouched at floor level and smiled again.

'Is someone looking after you?'

The girl nodded. 'Nanny,' she said. 'She's gone to get me a drink.'

Why was she in the emergency department? Sarah wondered. Did she have other complications from the terrible scarring her body had suffered? And why wasn't she in the main patient area? This room looked more like an office than an examination area now that she had time to look around. The desk area not taken up by a computer console was littered with paperwork and the end of the bed had what appeared to be male street clothes strewn across it. Was it, in fact, an area used by an on-call doctor? Somewhere to sleep at night if that waiting room ever emptied?

Also on the end of the bed was a sunhat that clearly belonged to the child sitting on the floor. Bright, artificial sunflowers decorated the straw brim but the hat was unusual because of what appeared to be a veil attached beneath the flowers. Good grief, was this little girl made to hide behind a veil when out in public? Was she also in this private room to be hidden away?

The moment or two Sarah took to make an impression of her surroundings was enough time for the child to think she might have forgotten about the shell. By the time Sarah looked back, it was tucked firmly in the girl's lap under two hands that were too small to cover it completely.

'It's pretty, isn't it?'

The nod was wary. Was Sarah about to ask for it back?

'What's your name?'

'Phoebe.'

'That's a pretty name.' Sarah smiled and after a moment's hesitation, Phoebe smiled back. At least, half her mouth smiled. The other half twisted in a painful movement that mirrored what was happening in Sarah's heart. She couldn't help herself. She had to reach out and stroke Phoebe's cheek. She didn't consciously choose the scarred side of her face, it just happened that way, but Phoebe didn't flinch. She stared back at Sarah with an expression of total amazement.

'Would you like to keep that shell, Phoebe?'

Phoebe nodded slowly, still staring at Sarah.

'Pretty,' she said finally.

Sarah nodded solemnly. 'Just like Phoebe.'

The curtain being flicked back seemed an intrusion on a very personal moment and Sarah was totally unprepared for the look of what could almost be fear on the face of the large Fijian woman standing there.

'Who are you? What are you doing here? You're not allowed here.'

'Sorry.' Sarah scrambled to her feet. 'My shell rolled in here by mistake. I just came to find it.'

'Find it and go.' The woman put a glass of water on the desk and held out her arms. Any misgivings Sarah had about Phoebe's 'nanny' vanished as she saw how eagerly the child went into the woman's embrace.

'Take shell,' Sarah was ordered. 'Go.'

'No, Nanny.' Phoebe twisted against an ample bosom. '*My* shell now.'

Sarah nodded as she backed away. 'It's a gift,' she explained. She ducked through the curtain swiftly, not wanting Phoebe to have the gift taken away. She could hear the small voice from the other side of the curtain.

'Pretty shell, Nanny. Phoebe's pretty, too.'

The response was in Fijian so Sarah had no chance to interpret it. She could only hope the woman would reinforce whatever boost Phoebe's self-esteem might have had. If the shell could serve as a reminder then it was far better with its new owner. Sadly, Phoebe would not have an easy road ahead in life but while Sarah could empathise to a startling degree, there was absolutely nothing she could do to help.

Maybe *this* was going to be the most lasting memory Sarah would have of this day. Something completely unrelated to her holiday or Tori's injury or Dr

Ben Dawson. A child who might have as much trouble as Sarah had had finding love in the world because the scarring made it harder for people to see who she was. Would it be any easier to have the scars on the outside, for everybody to see?

The distraction of the nurse coming back to find her was welcome. She had an orderly with her.

'The ambulance is ready to go to the airport now. We have come to help you with your bags.'

'Sarah—welcome back!'

'Thanks, Cathy.' Sarah sat down at the central desk in the paediatric ward's nurses' station with a smile for a good friend and a relieved glance at the wall clock. 'Six twenty-six. Thank goodness for that. I was sure I was going to be late.'

'Jet-lag, huh?'

'Hardly. I've been back for five days now.'

'What?'

'Didn't you hear about our disaster? Tori broke her leg. She's been up in Ward 16 since Wednesday though she's being discharged today. I would have thought you'd have heard about it by now.'

Cathy shook her head. 'I had three days off last week and it's been a madhouse in here since then. What happened?'

Other staff were rapidly filling the empty chairs in the area, ready for the staff change-over meeting. The ward's nurse manager, Christine, was heading for the whiteboard which looked alarmingly crowded with patient names and details.

'Long story,' Sarah whispered hurriedly. She pulled a small notebook and pen from her pocket. 'Tell you later.'

'Morning, all.' Christine's greeting signalled an end to any chatter. 'Looks like winter has really caught up with us over the weekend. We're two nurses short and we've got our annual RSV epidemic with four…' She checked the printout she was holding. 'No, five admissions yesterday. Sarah?' Christine's slightly worried expression was softened by a quick smile. 'Good to see you back. You've nursed Emerald Carson before, haven't you?'

'Oh, no! Is she an RSV victim?' Emerald had become a firm favourite with Sarah over many admissions due to complications from cystic fibrosis. Dealing with a bout of respiratory syncytial virus would be a lot harder for her.

Christine shook her head, looking grim. 'Looks more like pneumonia secondary to a viral infection. She's been in ICU over the weekend but they're ready to transfer her this morning. She'll be number one on your list for today.'

Sarah nodded, writing the name in her notebook. As if Emerald didn't have enough to cope with after the recent deterioration in her condition of needing insulin therapy for diabetes. She was such a darling. Too wise for her nine years but unconsciously determined to wring every moment of happiness out of what would undoubtedly be a short life. She was a child Sarah had taken to her heart from the first moment they'd met.

As Phoebe had been. Sarah had been quite correct in her guess that her meeting with the small, badly scarred girl would be a lasting memory. The poignant finale of that ill-fated holiday had stayed with her, haunting dreams and odd moments just as noticeably as the more turbulent impressions of Ben Dawson. Or the far more pleasant snatches of turquoise ocean, stunning sunsets, islanders singing, and twirling by firelight in a grass skirt with flowers in her hair.

'Sarah?' Christine's tone was less welcoming this time. 'Did you get that?'

'Kirsty James,' Cathy hissed. 'Croup.'

Sarah nodded. 'Kirsty,' she confirmed.

'I'll give you Shane Hayes as well. He's back again and on a course of IV penicillin. Looks like scarlet fever after that infection of his burn a couple of weeks ago. You may well end up with another case but I'm leaving a gap for any emergency admission.' Christine shook her head. 'Goodness knows, we're full up now but we'll just have to find the space if it's needed. Cathy? I'm putting you in the isolation room. All the RSV cases are contained and we really don't need this virus spreading through the ward. Visitors are restricted to close family only and...'

Christine's voice faded again as Sarah wrote Shane's name in her notebook. She'd nursed him on his initial admission as well, after he'd been badly scalded getting into an overly hot bath.

It must have been more than hot water that had caused Phoebe's burn. How much more scarring had her clothing covered? How much pain had the wee dot had to go through? Had her parents been there to comfort her or had that duty also been largely delegated to the nanny?

'Wakey-wakey.' Cathy was grinning as she stood up. 'Time to hit the deck.' She frowned. 'Guess I'll have to wait for lunch to hear about your holiday disaster. I'm going to be stuck in isolation.'

'I've got a feeling I'm going to be busy, too.' Sarah clipped the pen back into the pocket of the dark blue tunic she was wearing over matching trousers and any lapses in concentration were firmly dampened. This was getting back to reality and she was looking forward to it.

The nine-hour shift was, indeed, a very busy one. The hours flew past and there was no time to catch up with Cathy, but Sarah hardly noticed. She was caught up in the bustle and tension, the tears and laughter that working with sick children brought, and she loved it all.

Well, almost all of it. Parts of her day brought the kind of heartache that seemed to tie her ever more closely to her job. Like seeing Emerald almost choking as her physiotherapist helped her try and clear her lungs, which was never easy but far more distressing with the added burden of infection. Then Sarah had to provide the daunting number of her pancreatic enzyme supplement capsules to be swallowed before lunch. As unwell as she was, Emerald still hadn't lost her sense of humour.

'Don't know why I bother with lunch,' she told Sarah with a rueful smile. 'I have a whole plateful of pills.'

To add insult to injury, Sarah had to collect the supplies needed to test Emerald's blood-sugar levels and administer insulin.

'I can do this by myself now.' Emerald took the slim syringe from the tray with almost a flourish. 'Watch this, Sarah!'

Sarah watched and praised her patient. She was able to sit with her while her weary mother went to the hospital cafeteria for lunch and she had more than one cuddle during the day.

'I'm getting better,' Emerald announced that afternoon. 'My chest doesn't hurt so much any more. That's good, isn't it?'

'That's great, sweetheart.' Sarah knew her smile covered the painful squeeze of her heart. Emerald would never really get 'better', would she?

Six-month-old Kirsty would recover but her croup was severe enough to need oral dexamethasone and her mother was so distressed by her daughter's breathing difficulty she was having trouble coping. Whenever Sarah wasn't needed by Emerald or Shane, she found herself carrying Kirsty and giving the baby as much comfort as she could.

The barking cough, loud respiratory noises and even the miserable, grizzling cry couldn't put her off reaching for the infant to hold her. Christine was smiling when she saw Sarah rocking Kirsty and managing to fill in some of her paperwork at the same time.

'I wish everyone round here loved babies as much as you do.'

Sarah just returned the smile. She *did* love babies. She loved the challenge of caring for them and the reward of earning a smile or even a restful doze made her efforts worthwhile.

Shane Hayes wasn't smiling much, particularly after he managed to pull his IV line out. Sarah had to track down one of the overworked registrars and assist in replacing the line. They were shut into the treatment room with a bellowing toddler for what seemed like a very long time but the IV access necessary for delivering the aggressive antibiotic therapy was finally secured—taped down and splinted until the tiny arm all but vanished. Sarah's job satisfaction had certainly diminished thanks to the struggle and she felt more than weary.

'At least there's no way he's going to get this one out.'

'He'd better not.' The registrar sighed. 'We don't want a repeat performance, that's for sure.'

'No.' Sarah gathered Shane into her arms and his wailing subsided into hiccuping sobs. 'I'm off home in ten minutes, though. I'm sure it'll last that long.'

'Lucky you. I'm on duty till 10 p.m.'

Sarah didn't feel quite so lucky after she arrived home laden with shopping bags an hour later.

'Thank goodness you're back!' Tori was lying on the couch. 'I'm *so* bored!'

'How's the leg?'

'Sore.'

'Been up and about on your crutches?'

'Yeah. I can't manage the stairs yet, though.'

'You shouldn't have been trying.' Sarah dumped the grocery bags on the kitchen bench, wondering if she would have been better staying at home to supervise Tori. 'Had any visitors?'

'No.' Tori sighed heavily. 'It was more fun in hospital. Everyone had time to pop in there.'

'What have you been doing since you got back?' Sarah left the chicken and a selection of vegetables on the bench ready to do a stir-fry for dinner.

'I watched TV. The ''what to do if your boyfriend runs off with your mother'' kind of chat show.'

Sarah laughed. 'I knew there was a good reason to be in paid employment.'

'And then I found a good site on the internet. I put us both into a matchmaking outfit. Making up the profiles was fun.'

'Tori!' Sarah paused in her task of putting supplies into the pantry to shake her head.

'Don't worry. I disguised you as a twenty-two-year old, six-foot-tall blonde who works part time as a model. You had fifteen hits within an hour.'

'And you are?'

'Me.' Tori sighed again. 'I wanted to see whether anyone would be interested. All I got was one hit from a guy in Holland who's got a three-year-old kid. As if anyone's going to date someone with a kid!'

'Want a cup of tea?' Sarah flicked the switch on the electric jug. 'Are you due for any painkillers?'

'Yeah.'

'I wouldn't be put off by someone who had a child.' Preparations for dinner were left while Sarah curled up on the floor beside the couch, having produced mugs of tea for them both.

'You can have the guy from Holland, then.'

'No, thanks.' Flirting in cyberspace held no appeal whatsoever. The man in question was hardly likely to be tall and tanned or have gorgeously dark hair and eyes, was he?

'How was work?'

'Busy.' Sarah sipped her tea. 'There's some great kids in, though. Emerald's back. The little girl with CF, remember?'

'The one who's got diabetes now?'

'Mmm. She's got pneumonia at the moment, poor wee thing.'

'Will she survive?'

'She's improving…for now.'

Tori broke the heavy silence that fell. 'You shouldn't get so involved, you know, Sas. You break your heart over those kids. Maybe you should come and work in Emergency. When you only see them for a short while you don't get that kind of involvement.'

'But that's what I love about the job.' Sarah wriggled closer to the gas fire. 'Cold, isn't it?'

'Freezing. This house is way too old and too big. Maybe we should sell it.'

Sarah's glance was startled. 'What?'

'It must be worth a fortune by now. Mum and Dad bought it thirty years ago when nobody wanted to live this far from the city. We've got the beach just down the road and the bush behind us. We could be millionaires if we sold up.'

'You're not serious, are you, Tori? You've never lived anywhere else.'

'No. I'm just feeling down. I'm bored and my leg hurts…and I've been thinking about Mum a lot today. I just wish she was here to look after me.'

'I shouldn't have let you talk me out of taking more time off and staying home.'

'We need the money,' Tori reminded her. 'We spent all our savings on that holiday and I hate to think what the gas bill is going to be like this month.'

Another silence fell. Neither of them wanted to contemplate how much of their savings had been wasted by the way that holiday had ended.

'I love this house,' Sarah said quietly a minute or two later. 'It's the only home I ever really had.'

'Feels too empty now.'

'Mmm.' Sarah thought back to the days before Carol's high blood pressure and other problems had made her cut back on fostering children. To the time when she had always seemed to have a baby on one hip or toddlers playing in the rambling garden. She'd preferred the little ones, and Sarah had been an ex-

ception, both for her age and the length of time she
had stayed. Even though a formal adoption had never
been implemented, Tori hadn't questioned the fair-
ness of Sarah inheriting half the house. She had been
part of the family from the moment she'd set foot on
the old polished floorboards.

'Mum was amazing, wasn't she?' Tori was smiling
as she settled back more comfortably on her cushions.
'I should have been jealous of sharing her with so
many other kids but I never was. She always had time
to make me feel special.'

'Me, too.'

'Some of them were really hard work. I couldn't
have done it.'

'I could.' Sarah wrapped her arms around her knees
and stared into the glow of the fire.

'But some of the problems they had! The bedwet-
ting, and being scared of the dark. There was that boy
in the wheelchair for a while, too. Craig. I mean, it
would be hard enough if they were your own children.'

'I had problems, too,' Sarah reminded her. 'And if
those children weren't getting what they needed in
their own homes, they needed it even more from
Carol. I think it's easier to love kids that need so
much. Especially the ones with real problems.' Like
small, scarred Phoebe could have. She would need so
much love and support to help her get past the barriers
her appearance would create. 'I could do it,' she re-
peated, almost to herself. 'In fact, I'd really like to
do it.'

'You need to have your own children first.'

'Maybe I won't get the chance to have my own
children.'

'Don't be daft. Even if you didn't find anyone you wanted to marry, you could still have a child or two.'

'What, just pick some guy and get pregnant?'

'It's been done before.'

Sarah shook her head. 'I couldn't do that.'

'You could, if you didn't throw opportunities away. You could have had Ben Dawson, no trouble, and just think how cute one of his babies would have been.'

Sarah didn't want to think about Ben or his potential offspring. He was simply part of a fantasy she would probably be revisiting for the rest of her life. One that was going to make it even less probable that she would find a father for children of her own. But maybe that was not going to be the handicap she feared. Maybe there was a way around it.

'Carol got paid quite well for fostering, didn't she?'

'Well, she never worked and we always had enough to eat.'

'She was single, too.'

'Widowed, but, yeah.'

'I could do it,' Sarah murmured.

'Do what?'

'Foster kids. Lots of people don't want to take the ones with physical problems. Like CF, for instance. Or…or maybe a kid that's badly scarred for some reason. I'd take them.'

'Are you serious? What about your job? You love nursing.'

'Because I love the kids. How much better would it be if I could care for them without having to watch them have surgery or painful procedures? If I could take them to school instead of down to the treatment room? Put them to bed with a story and a cuddly toy instead of an extra dose of morphine?'

'You want to fill this house up with kids?'

Sarah bit her lip. 'You're right. I couldn't do that to you. It's really your house more than mine.'

'Don't be daft.' Tori's eyes were drifting shut. 'And why should I mind, anyway? It's what was happening here for most of my life. If that's what you really want to do, Sas, you go for it.' One eye opened. 'Just don't expect me to be changing nappies or babysitting every time you want to go out.'

'I wouldn't.' Sarah got slowly to her feet. Tori's painkillers were clearly kicking in and a rest while she prepared dinner seemed like a good idea. Sarah had plenty to think about anyway.

The idea of fostering children was better than good. It shone with the brilliance of genuine treasure. Perhaps she had just discovered what she needed to do with her life to gain ultimate fulfilment.

She could forget tropical islands and gorgeous men who would never be interested if they really got to know her. She wouldn't forget Phoebe, though. She had been the inspiration and Sarah knew she was going to follow this path.

She would take the very first step tomorrow.

CHAPTER FIVE

'I'M SORRY.'

She didn't *look* sorry. Sarah stared speechlessly at the woman seated on the other side of a desk piled high with manila folders. The closed folder directly in front of her had Sarah's name on it and contained a sheaf of papers she had spent many hours painstakingly filling in, nearly a month ago now.

Faced with Sarah's silent and disbelieving stare, the woman sighed and reopened the folder.

'We can go over it if you like but I think it's a waste of time. Yours *and* mine. You're simply not suitable as a foster-parent.'

'Why not?'

Another sigh implied that the social welfare department's representative had too great a choice of starting points.

'You're too young.'

'I'm thirty. I'm quite old enough to know what I want to do with my life. There are plenty of thirty-year-olds who are raising several children.'

'And if *you* were in that position, you would have a much better chance of being eligible.'

'Maybe I'm in a better position to care for foster-children because I don't have children of my own competing for attention.'

'But you have no experience.'

'How can you say that? I'm a nurse. I started out in Theatre but I've been in paediatrics for the last four years. I work with children every day. I care for new-born babies and teenagers and every age in between.'

'Being a parent—even on a temporary basis—is a very different proposition.'

'I know that.' Sarah was trying very hard to keep her tone reasonable. Persuasive even. 'That's *why* I want to be a foster-parent.'

'All right.' The woman pushed her spectacles up as she pinched the bridge of her nose. 'Here's another reason. You say that you're prepared to give up your source of income, but you have no other means of support.'

'I can manage. I worked it out. I live in a house I half own so I don't have to pay rent or a mortgage. The reimbursement for fostering is more than adequate, especially if I take on more than one child.'

The huff of expelled breath was almost laughter. 'Just how many children did you envisage caring for?'

'Only one or two to start with,' Sarah said quietly.

'And then?'

'That would depend on their ages and their needs.' Deliberately unclenching the fists her hands had unconsciously formed, Sarah took a deep breath. Maybe this was a test to see how serious she was. If she gave up at the first obstacle, she certainly wouldn't be considered suitable, would she?

'I was fourteen when I went to live with Carol Preston,' she said. 'I was expected to help with the younger children in the house and it was that kind of family life and being given those kind of responsibilities that made all the difference. If I could do that for even one other child I would feel like I'd achieved something very worthwhile.' It felt like a minor victory to be holding eye contact with this official.

'I know I could give them the kind of environment and love they need. Maybe I know that better than any of the more "suitable" applicants because I've been there.' Sarah had to clear her throat. 'I know what it's like to *be* one of those children.'

Something had changed. The woman was smiling. 'Carol Preston was a legend in this department,' she told Sarah. 'She was always there in an emergency. She could always fit one more in. We've missed her.'

Sarah's eyes misted. 'I wouldn't say I'd ever be able to take her place. All I'm asking for is a chance to try.'

The headshake was far more sympathetic this time. 'I can't give you that, Sarah. Not yet. I'm sorry.'

'But you haven't given me a good reason. There are no criteria that I fail to meet. I don't have a police record, I'm in good health, I have my own home, I—'

'You're single.'

'That's not necessarily an exclusion. It *said* so, on the form. Carol was single.'

'Widowed. That's different.'

'*Why?*'

'You're far too young and intelligent and beautiful to have given up on meeting someone, Sarah.'

'What's that got to do with it?'

'You'll get married one of these days. You'll have children of your own.'

'Even if I did, I'd still want to take in foster-children. Anyone who loved me enough to marry me would accept that because it's what I want to do with my life.'

'If that's the case, come back when you *are* married. Bring your husband with you. If you both feel the same way, we'd be delighted to go further in the process of screening you as foster-parents.' Eyebrows rose in curiosity. 'Is there someone on the horizon maybe?'

'No.' The tone was more blunt than Sarah had intended but frustration and disappointment were gaining ground. 'So you're saying that if I don't get married I've got no show of being accepted?'

'If you still feel the same way in, say, ten years' time and you have a stable and secure home situation, it probably won't make any difference if you haven't got a partner.'

'Ten years! I'll be *forty*!'

'You'll be someone with a lot more life experience and you'll really know what it is you're looking to achieve with your life. It's hardly too old to start being a mother, you know. Carol must have been well into her forties by the time you went to live with her.' Her face and tone softened enough to make Sarah revise her opinion of this woman's suitability for her job. 'You've got so much going for you, Sarah. Don't close off your options too soon. There's not many people who would have quite the same generosity of spirit that you obviously have. I'd hate to think you might miss out on finding your soul mate because you were putting other people's children first in your life.'

'If he was my soul mate, he'd feel the same way,' Sarah muttered.

'Not necessarily. I love kids but I wouldn't take on someone else's by choice. That doesn't make me a bad person.'

'You'd take them on if you really loved him.'

'Only if they were his kids and I had no choice, and that's *not* going to happen.' Tori was clearly tired of a conversation that had been aired more than once. 'If they have kids, it's enough to put me off. I had too much of it while I was growing up, I guess. I've got nothing against children but it's made me appreciate my freedom. I want some time to have fun with the man I marry and you can't have fun with rugrats in tow. Are you ready to go yet?'

'It's only two o'clock. I've got an hour before my shift starts.'

'I said I'd get in at 2.30.'

'Are you sure about this, Tori? You only got the walking brace yesterday.'

'I'm fine. They're so short-staffed in Emergency they were delighted when I offered to come in. I'm only going to have light duties and I can go home when I need to.' Tori was already limping towards the door with determination. 'I'll probably only be sitting at a desk on the phone, trying to find beds for patients or something, but it'll be a damn sight better than sitting at home. I'm going mad, Sas. I need something to do. Something *real*.'

Sarah picked up her car keys and followed Tori. 'You and me both,' she muttered. But she'd hit a brick wall with the 'something real' she wanted to do and there didn't seem to be any way to get around it.

Emerald had gone home two weeks ago, happily with her lung function only marginally worse following her bout of pneumonia, but there were plenty more small patients ready to worm their way into permanent residence in Sarah's heart.

Carlos was an engaging three-year-old with mild cerebral palsy affecting one side of his body, a higher than normal level of intelligence and a smile that could light up a whole room. He was due for surgery the next day to correct a deformity in his affected ankle that was making it impossible for him to use the heel of his foot for walking.

With one foot on tiptoe and an uncooperative arm, Carlos had a curious, lurching gait but still managed an impressive speed. His affected arm was even more of a nuisance due to its irregular and involuntary movements but Carlos actually managed to find the situation amusing as long as he didn't hurt himself.

The requested drink of juice that Sarah provided on her first meeting with Carlos was knocked flying.

'Oops!' His following gurgle of laughter was totally infectious and Sarah was smitten.

Jenny, the toddler's mother, was very apologetic. She grabbed a towel to mop Sarah's uniform.

'I'm so sorry,' she said. 'Carlos doesn't really think it's funny to get someone wet, do you, Carlos?'

Sarah was laughing herself. 'I know he didn't do it on purpose. It's not a problem, honestly. I often get far worse things on my uniform than juice.'

Jenny stopped mopping. 'I don't suppose he's going to be laughing much tomorrow anyway. After the operation.'

Sarah smiled reassuringly at the anxious mother. 'You'll be surprised how fast he'll bounce back. We'll make sure he's not in too much pain, don't worry.'

'His dad's coming in for the day as well. Will we both be allowed to stay with him?'

'Daddy!' Carlos beamed. 'Daddy's coming too.'

'You'll be allowed to go up to Theatre with him.' Sarah turned towards her patient again. 'You get the special bed tomorrow, Carlos. Come on, I'll show it to you.'

This particular hospital bed had its cot sides disguised by wooden panels, shaped and painted to make it look like a bright red racing car and had been a huge success in making a trip to Theatre an exciting privilege for small children.

'Wanna ride!'

'In the morning, Carlos,' Sarah promised. 'Shall we go and find you some more juice now?' The fact that Jenny was trying to control a rather wobbly lip, having viewed the car, had not gone unnoticed.

'We'll have a chat to the anaesthetist when he comes to visit Carlos this afternoon. If it's Chris, I know you'll be welcome to stay with Carlos until he's asleep and then you can be there again when he wakes up in Recovery.'

'And if it's not him?'

'You might have to let him go into the anaesthetic room with the nurses but he'll be sleepy, having had some medication, and the staff up there are well used to looking after children. He'll be fine, honestly.'

'Will you be here?'

'I'm on an afternoon shift again so it'll all be over by the time I get here.' Sarah caught Carlos just before he lurched into the path of an oncoming trolley. She swung him up into her arms, which elicited a squeal of glee. 'I'll be looking forward to seeing that smile again when I come back tomorrow.'

She did get a smile from Carlos the next day but it was a very sleepy one. In a room on his own for the moment, Carlos lay quietly on his bed with his parents sitting, hand in hand, beside him. They both had their other hands touching their son.

'Is there anything you need?' Sarah found herself edging back towards the door with a totally uncharacteristic desire to find something else to do. 'Can I get you both a cup of tea?'

'We're fine, thanks.'

Cathy poked her head around the door. 'Sarah? You're needed. Juliette's had a bit of an accident.'

It was only a short walk up the ward to Juliette's room but it was long enough for Sarah to identify the unpleasant emotion she had just experienced. An even more chilling thought was that it could be a glimpse into her own future. Was she going to start feeling envious of other people's children and their family bonds? Would envy become jealousy and possibly poison her soul until she lost the joy of even working with these children?

No. It couldn't happen. Sarah would not allow it to happen. As if to prove it, she gave Juliette's mother the most cheerful smile she could summon through the window before gowning up to enter the room.

Five-month-old Juliette had gastroenteritis severe enough to have left her dehydrated and requiring IV fluids. The bug had still not run its course and Sarah had a nasty mess to clean up in the cot. Having washed and changed the baby, with a non-stop commentary of soothing chatter to try and make up for having her face covered by a mask, Sarah handed her back to her mother for a cuddle and breastfeed. She bundled all the dirty linen into a red bio-hazard laundry bag and excused herself to deliver the bag to the sluice room and find new linen for the cot.

The few minutes in her own company forced Sarah

to examine the realisation that had made her want to flee from the sight of Carlos and his parents. The lingering disappointment from that interview with the woman at the social welfare department was not something she could rationally cling to. The woman had been quite right. It was far better for children to be in a real family situation and ideally that included two parents who had children of their own.

Yes, Carol had been single but she'd had a child of her own and the house had been permeated with reminders that they'd once been a complete and happy family unit. The piano was still cluttered with photographs of Tori as a baby, being held aloft playing 'aeroplanes', being pushed in a swing as a toddler or walking hand in hand with a tall man who seemed to be always laughing.

And, more than once, Sarah had paused to examine a wedding photograph, struck by the expressions on the faces of Carol and Tom as they laughed into each other's eyes.

Sarah did have the right to feel disappointed. Deflated. Even despairing. But she needed to be honest with herself here. Maybe the real disappointment wasn't that she had failed in a bid to foster children but because she was failing in something much more important. The dream of finding the soul mate that woman had gently mentioned, having babies of their own and making a family that was so secure and loving that it had the potential to include other, less fortunate children.

Sarah buried her nose in her armful of clean linen, inhaling the fresh scent. Then she straightened her spine and moved back through the ward. She would sort out Juliette's bed and then she would go and spend some time with Carlos. His parents would need a break at some point and Sarah would be there to take their place.

If Carlos was subdued for the rest of that duty, so was Sarah. Little by little she accepted that the last few weeks had provided an insight that might be painful but had to be faced before she could move on. She had to deal with something very personal before she could hope to get what she wanted out of life.

The notion of fostering children had been a red herring. Had its starting point been meeting Phoebe or had meeting Phoebe simply provided an escape from the turmoil that meeting Ben Dawson had sparked? The experiences of the last few weeks had been unsettling to say the least and Sarah felt sadly older and wiser. By the time she left the ward to go and collect Tori, Sarah was more than ready to head home. She needed the security of being in the place she felt she belonged more than anywhere else. The bonus of Tori's virtually limitless optimism wouldn't go astray either.

Except that Tori had a sparkle in her eyes that filled Sarah with misgiving.

'You look like you've been enjoying yourself.'

'I have. It's been great fun.'

'How's the leg holding up?'

'It's a bit sore.'

'Are you tired?'

'Exhausted.'

'So what are you looking so pleased about, then?'

Tori grinned as she fastened her seatbelt for the drive home. 'I thought you'd never ask. I've found him, Sas. He's *perfect*!'

'Uh-oh!' But Sarah was grinning as she groaned. 'Don't tell me, it's the father of your babies, right?'

'Nope. This one's for you, Sas. I wouldn't touch him with a bargepole.'

'Oh, cheers! I suppose he's four feet tall and has terrible halitosis.'

'No, he's actually very good-looking. He's a para-medic and he's just started working on the road here. His name's Matthew and he's English, kind of. I found him having a coffee in the staffroom and we got talking.'

Sarah smiled at the thought of the poor man responding to a barrage of Tori's questions.

'How can you be "kind of" English?' She turned out of the car park, deliberately stamping on the memory of where she'd last heard an English accent. Ben hadn't been 'kind of' English, though, had he? He'd described himself as a 'Londoner, through and through'.

'Well, his parents live in Auckland but he went to England when he'd finished university and ended up training as an ambulance officer there. It had something to do with his much older sister marrying a British medic.'

'So he's too old for you, is that it?'

'He's thirty-two. Hardly geriatric.'

'So what's wrong with him?'

'He's got four kids. *Four!* And they're not even his! I thought of you as soon as he started telling me about them.'

Despite herself, Sarah's heart missed a beat. Was this fate stepping in via Tori again? Another life-changing episode coming up? 'Whose children are they?'

'His sister's. She and her husband were killed in a car accident in January. There was no one to take them so Matthew's adopted them all. He's brought them back here to live because he thinks New Zealand is a better place to grow up. He also wanted them to be closer to their grandparents.'

'He must be a nice guy.' Anyone who could do that much for the sake of children had to be an interesting person.

'He's *very* nice,' Tori said firmly. 'If it weren't for those kids, I'd be tempted myself.'

'Is he single?'

'You bet. His girlfriend gave him an ultimatum of her or the kids. He chose the kids obviously. He was quite philosophical about it really. Said he knew it was unlikely he'd find a woman interested in him now. I said, "You never know", and he gave me this funny look.' Tori chuckled wickedly. 'I had to tell him not to get the wrong idea here. *I* wasn't some kind of saint but they were out there.'

'And then you started talking about me, I suppose.'

'Nope. He got called to an arrest but I wasn't going to say anything, anyway. Honest!'

'Hmm.' Sarah almost missed the turnoff from the motorway. '*Four* of them, you said?' Talk about an instant family.

'Yep. The oldest is a teenage girl and there's twins at the bottom. A boy and girl who are about seven. There's another boy in between.'

'Maybe I should drop into Emergency and say hello.'

'You won't need to.' Tori sounded suspiciously smug and Sarah's head turned sharply.

'Victoria Preston! What have you done *this* time?'

'Matthew's an expert in USAR stuff.'

The apparent change of subject made Sarah blink. 'Urban search and rescue?'

'That's the one. He's running a weekend introductory course and is trying to recruit medical staff who might be interested in making themselves available for callouts. I've put both our names down.'

'*What?*'

'I checked your roster on the computer. You've got next weekend free.'

'You could have asked me first!'

'If I'd asked, you would have just thought up an excuse not to do it.' Tori sounded unrepentant. 'You'd spend your weekend moping about and doing housework or gardening or something.'

'I don't mope!'

'You do on the inside. 'Fess up, Sas! You've been less than happy ever since we got back from Fiji and not being allowed to be a foster-mother has made things a lot worse, hasn't it?' Tori didn't wait for a response. 'A challenge is exactly what you need. Something a bit different. Even if you don't like Matthew, you'll enjoy the course. There's lots of us going. It'll be *fun*.'

'This sounds suspiciously like the arguments you used to get me to agree to go to Fiji.' Sarah turned off the road onto the tree-lined driveway that led to their home. 'That didn't end up being much fun, did it?'

'It was until I broke my stupid leg.'

'And what about your leg? How can you do a rescue course with a brace on, or is it all classroom stuff?'

'No, there's a practical session in a rubbish dump

or somewhere. Matt says I can be the patient.' Tori
opened the car door and grimaced as she moved her
leg. 'Come on, Sas. If I can do it with a sore leg,
you've got no excuse.'

Except for the sensation of being steamrollered.
Pushed towards something else that fate had in store
for her. Sarah sighed. Maybe she should just go with
the flow.

'All right. I'll come.'

It was the best decision Sarah had made in what
seemed a very long time. Tori had been right on more
than one count. Sarah did need something new in her
life. The course was fascinating and Matthew
Buchanan *was* a very nice guy.

The two-day USAR awareness course was intensive and covered a lot of ground. Not enough for any
of them to qualify as a USAR technician, but
Matthew hoped that some of the group of nurses, ambulance officers and doctors would be keen enough
to enrol for more extensive training. If they weren't,
the understanding of some of the principles of USAR
would make them valuable extras if called in as support to an urban search and rescue operation.

Sarah's interest was captured right from the start,
when Matthew used a slide show to remind them of
just how many incidents had occurred recently and
had needed the kind of expertise USAR could provide. The images of earthquakes, landslides, terrorist
bombings and plane crashes were chilling.

'Don't think it could never happen and. involve
you,' Matthew warned the group. 'We've had major
flooding and then a series of earthquakes in the Bay
of Plenty in the last few weeks and it was just lucky

that houses got evacuated before the landslides started. There's a cyclone warning in place in the Pacific, threatening Rarotonga and possibly Fiji at the moment. If they need assistance, New Zealand will be the first port of call.'

Would it ever be possible to hear a reference to Fiji without immediately thinking of Ben Dawson? Sarah tried not to, of course. She tried very hard but it only seemed to make it more impossible.

Matthew had a kind of laid-back personality and confidence that also reminded her of Ben. She could easily have been distracted into making further comparisons if the things he was talking about hadn't been so interesting.

'Situational hazards include what's below the debris, like flooding, toxic or flammable environments and different levels of elevation. On the surface you could have a piece of rubble weighing anything up to several tonnes. You might have to deal with protruding reinforcing bars, electrical cables, glass or nails.'

Tori caught Sarah's eye and smiled. She looked like a magician who had pulled a rabbit out of a hat and Sarah knew it was because she was looking so interested. She rolled her eyes but smiled back and found, to her consternation, that the small interchange had been noticed by Matthew. He didn't appear annoyed by any lapse in concentration, however. He smiled himself before continuing.

'Weather conditions on the surface could be anything from snow and ice to hurricane-force winds. Overhead hazards could be something being lifted away by a crane or sections of walls or ceilings that are unstable. "Look up and live", as we say.'

Yes, Matthew was clearly a nice person. He was

also as good-looking as Tori had promised. Brown hair, rather than black. Hazel eyes rather than dark brown. Knowing what she did about his personal life, Sarah should have found him irresistible, but even though she tried to feel attracted, it was a losing battle.

She listened attentively, learning about rubble crawls and line-and-hail searches. She participated wholeheartedly in the practical exercise the next day at a hard-fill rubbish tip on the outskirts of town. Tori had been hidden, buried beneath sheets of corrugated iron, plasterboard and planks. Sarah joined the human chain as they crawled slowly up the huge mound of debris.

'Rescue team above. Can you hear me?'

'Nothing heard.'

Matthew was the safety officer and encouraged the group constantly.

'Remember to always have three points of contact with the rubble. Move slowly and carefully. Watch out for any identified hazard and for any that I've missed marking with the paint.'

It was Sarah who heard the first faint call from Tori. She remembered to raise her arm and point in the direction the sound was coming from, and earned praise from Matthew. He made a point of coming up to her after the exercise as well.

'That was brilliant, Sarah. You led the assessment and management of the patient your group found perfectly.'

'Thanks. I enjoyed it.'

'I hope we'll see you again, then. On another course maybe?'

'Sure, I'd be keen.'

Tori overheard the last part of the conversation but her delight was dampened after they got home on the Sunday night and she had to accept that it was the content of the course and not the instructor that had captured Sarah's interest.

'But what's *wrong* with him?'

'Absolutely nothing. He's a lovely person.'

'He likes *you*.'

'I like him, too.'

'So what's the problem? He's perfect.'

Sarah shook her head. 'Sorry, not for me.'

'But why not?'

'I just don't feel attracted to him. Not in that way.'

'You don't know him properly yet.'

'Weren't you the one that said if you found the right person you had at least an inkling of it the first moment you met them?'

'And you shot me down in flames! *You* said that any funny feelings were just a twinge of lust and that you couldn't fall in love until you'd known someone long enough to trust them.'

'Yeah…well…' Sarah shifted uncomfortably on the couch and reached for the television remote.

'Well, what?'

'That was before.'

'Before *what*?'

'Oh…all *right*,' Sarah growled, muting the sound on the television. 'It was before Ben Dawson kissed me. Satisfied?'

Tori's mouth opened and closed but no sound emerged.

Sarah grinned. 'Hey, does this remote work on you as well? Wicked!'

'Why didn't you *tell* me?' Tori gasped. 'How you felt about Ben?'

'I thought I'd be able to forget about it faster if I didn't talk about it.' Sarah sighed heavily. 'I had no idea I wouldn't be able to forget at all. Or that I'd be comparing every other man I met to him. Or that whatever that weird feeling was it would somehow get stronger instead of disappearing.'

'You're in love with him,' Tori breathed. 'Oh... *Sas*!'

'I can't be. I barely know the man.'

'You'd better get to know him, then.'

'Oh, sure! How am I supposed to do that?' Even talking about the possibility of seeing Ben again gave Sarah a twinge that sent odd tingles like an electric current running through her.

'Take another holiday.'

Sarah snorted. 'He couldn't wait to see the back of us last time.'

'Maybe that's because I was flirting with him and it was *you* he was interested in.'

'Hmm.' Could that have been the cause of the hostility? Had Tori's drug-induced confession that Sarah hadn't been interested and had handed him on to Tori been enough to spark that anger? If she'd been in his place, she would have been offended as well—particularly if the interest on his side had been genuine.

'It's too late now.' And what about those initially strong impressions Sarah had had of the man? Ben's competence in treating Tori and the serious side of his nature that had been apparent didn't prove he wasn't a dropout in search of an easy lifestyle and a great sex life.

'No, it's not.'

'We can't afford another holiday—and anyway, look at that!' Sarah pointed at images of tropical islands on the news bulletin. Palm trees were bending in dangerously high winds. Buildings and huts had been flattened. She fumbled for the remote. It couldn't be the Fijian islands, could it? The map that appeared, showing the path of the cyclone, made it look as though the worst affected area was further north. Samoa or the Solomons perhaps? Was Ben involved?

Frustratingly, the bulletin finished just as the sound came on.

'I wonder if it's hitting Fiji.' Tori was still staring at the screen. 'Ring Matthew and tell him you could be available as part of any USAR team that gets sent over.'

'As if!'

'Don't think it could never happen and involve *you*,' Tori quipped.

Almost as she finished speaking, the telephone started ringing. Tori actually went a shade paler.

'It's for you,' she whispered. 'This is *it*, Sas, I know it is.'

'Oh, rot!'

But Sarah's grin faded and her heart was pounding as she reached to answer the phone.

CHAPTER SIX

'EVER been in a Hercules before?'

Sarah nodded and then had to shout over the engine noise. 'A few weeks ago, actually. My sister broke her leg in Fiji and we came out on an army flight.'

It was no less uncomfortable this time, sitting on bench seats in the fuselage of the huge, lumbering aircraft, with the bulk of space taken up by box after box of medical supplies.

'I've never done this before, though.'

'What's that?' The young, bearded doctor seated beside Sarah was a stranger from another Auckland hospital.

'Been on a relief medical team.'

'It's hard work,' he shouted back. 'But very satisfying. I'm Kevin, by the way. General surgical registrar.'

'Pleased to meet you, Kevin. I'm Sarah. We'll be based at Suva hospital, won't we?' That had been the deciding factor for Sarah when she had received that unexpected phone call asking if she could be available as part of a medical team to help with the Pacific island emergency. Excitement at the opportunity to see Ben again had pushed aside any nervousness about accepting such a challenge.

'We'll be split up. Some of us are going to Nadi or Lautoka.'

Suva was the capital of Fiji and its major hospital was where Tori had been treated, but Sarah had no

idea how far from Nadi or Lautoka it was, or how
large the hospitals in the other towns might be. Then
again, she had no idea what kind of role a GP who
looked after holiday resorts might be expected to take
in such a crisis.

Maybe Ben was touring around smaller islands, sta-
bilising patients and deciding who needed to be evacuated to hospital. He would be there somewhere,
though, wouldn't he? And she'd be a lot closer than
she had been in New Zealand.

'What will we have to do?'

'Just what you do at home basically—with way too
many patients and not nearly enough space or gear.
Forget about sleep. Or decent food or even a hot
shower.' He grinned. 'You'll love it.'

Sarah's face creased into an expression of doubt
but she gave up the effort of conversing over the engine noise. She also gave up any fantasies of working
side by side with Ben, saving lives in peril thanks to
the aftermath of a relentlessly severe tropical storm
that had brought major damage and flooding to many
areas and a tidal wave that had claimed at least one
low-lying island.

It was thirty-six hours since the storm had struck,
but the airport at Nadi had only just reopened and
conditions were still rough as the military plane
ploughed its way through the night sky. Strong gusts
of wind buffeted the passengers as they disembarked
and it was still raining. There were no garlands of
exotic flowers or smiling islanders to greet her this
time, and Sarah had to hurry out of the way of a
forklift heading towards the open back of the plane's
fuselage.

'This way, Sarah!' Kevin caught her arm and they

hurried towards two trucks that marked the collection point for the team.

There were twenty of them, all doctors or nurses who had been sent with the medical supplies from New Zealand. While it was thanks to Sarah's attendance at the USAR awareness course that her name had appeared on the database, USAR itself hadn't been activated. Most victims were readily accessible and the major problem for the islands appeared to be a lack of resources to cope with the sheer number of injured.

A man in army fatigues was sorting the group. 'We need another doctor and nurse for Suva,' he called.

Kevin stepped forward. 'I'll go.'

Hadn't Ben said he worked two days a week at a hospital in Suva? She moved to follow Kevin.

'I'm a nurse,' she told the co-ordinator. 'Sarah Mitchell. I'm happy to go to Suva.'

'Great. Climb aboard.' He thumped the side of the truck as she clambered over the backboard and Sarah virtually fell into a sitting position as the vehicle jerked into motion.

'Fun already, isn't it?' Kevin helped her regain her balance.

Sarah grinned. That curious excitement was building again, even more strongly now she was here. The murky dawn struggling to appear through a curtain of drizzle as they reached the large township of Suva bore no resemblance to Sarah's memories of Fiji, but somewhere—maybe in the very direction she was heading—was the man who seemed to have claimed a rather large part of her mind. Or heart. Possibly both.

Fate had stepped in and with the contribution of

Tori's eloquently persuasive efforts, her decision to take advantage of the opportunity had seemed preordained. Now that she had embarked on this journey, Sarah had every intention of, at the very least, sorting out what was going on in her head.

The first steps into the hospital complex were made eagerly, but any notion of meeting Ben Dawson's gaze over a line of tidily arranged beds vanished as soon as Sarah set foot inside and she was forced to negotiate the chaos to follow the other members of her team.

It was impossible to even distinguish staff members among the crowds of people. Patients and their relatives were lying on floors, propped up against walls or just milling about, with children being held in the arms of adults. One corridor had a line of mattresses stretching down one side, and for every patient lying down there had to be two or three other people nearby.

Sarah saw blood-soaked bandages and wounds that should have been covered but weren't. There were faces twisted in pain and the cries of frightened and miserable children could be heard constantly. She was almost too shocked to register any disappointment that the man waiting to brief her team wasn't Dr Dawson.

The grey-haired Indian man introduced himself as the medical director of the hospital, Dr Singh.

'Thank you all very much for volunteering,' he said with a warm smile. 'You are the first group of professional aid to arrive and we are very relieved to see you.'

His smile faded. 'As you will have heard, we are overwhelmed with the numbers of injured requiring both surgery and nursing care. We will be able to start airlifting some victims now that the airports are open again, but it will take some time to get on top of the crisis. We still have some islands that are cut off so we really have no idea how many more patients will need attention in the next few days.'

Sarah found herself distracted as he went on to give a brief description of the devastation the storm had wrought. Was Ben's island cut off? Could he be injured and unable to gain assistance or even let anyone know what had happened? No. He'd had a satellite phone. Someone would know. Maybe Dr Singh, who was now explaining that the army was providing tents which would be erected in the hospital grounds to provide accommodation for the emergency relief teams. She could ask him, perhaps, as soon as this meeting was over.

'Most of the cases have been trauma so far, of course,' Dr Singh went on. 'People have been hit by debris carried in flood waters or by the wind. Some were still trapped inside their houses when the buildings were destroyed. Already, though, we are seeing some cases of infection and this will become more of a problem over the next few days. Water supplies have also been disrupted and the first cases of gastroenteritis are coming in.'

Dr Singh sighed wearily. 'We have been short of beds and staff, equipment and drugs. We have three operating theatres here and they have been in use twenty-four hours a day, but the queues are still growing. We are all very tired.'

A woman entered the room as he began a roll-call. Dr Singh scanned the list in his hand then looked up at the group.

'Sarah Mitchell? Are you present?'

'Yes.' Sarah stood up, her heart thumping erratically. Who was asking for her? And why? Had a list been circulated prior to their arrival? Was Ben expecting her...wanting to talk to her?

'It says here that you have experience as a theatre nurse—is that correct?'

'Yes, but I've been in paediatrics for the last four years.'

Dr Singh waved his hand as though such a detail was not of any importance under the circumstances. 'Could you go with Elena now, please? They're desperately short-staffed in Theatre 2.'

'Sure.' Sarah hesitated and reached for the small back pack containing the personal items she had been advised to bring.

'Take it with you.' Dr Singh nodded. 'Someone will make sure you know where to go when you get a break. Is Kevin Fielder also here?'

'Yes.'

'You're a surgical registrar, yes?'

'That's right.'

'Can you go with Elena as well, please? The surgeon in Theatre 2 requires an assistant.'

Sarah was thankful she had a now familiar face with her as she hurried to keep up with their guide.

'Are you a nurse, Elena?'

'Yes.' The young woman turned a corner and led them up a staircase. 'I was supposed to be on vacation but everyone needs to help just now. It's been terrible.'

More mattresses lined the corridor leading to the small theatre suite and Sarah was horrified to see how unwell some of these people looked. She saw twisted limbs and bleeding that looked poorly controlled. People who had to be relatives were holding bags of IV fluid aloft and a woman was crying softly as she cradled a small girl with a badly traumatised face.

She shouldn't be here, Sarah thought with sudden conviction. Her selfish agenda of wanting to see Ben again seemed frivolous against such a backdrop. How on earth could they be expected to try and help *so* many people?

Kevin must have read her expression as she turned to glance again at the length of the corridor.

'We only treat one person at a time,' he reminded her. 'We just have to do the best we can.'

Sarah nodded. Then she took a very deep breath. The reasons why she had agreed to come were irrelevant now. She *could* do this, and she was going to do it to the very best of her ability.

The surgeon currently working in Theatre 2 was an Australian, Richard Dean, who had been on holiday in Fiji with his family.

'Some holiday, huh?' He was delighted to see both Kevin and Sarah dressed in theatre clothing. 'You're a nurse, aren't you, Sarah? Happy to scrub?'

Sarah nodded, reaching for soap and a nailbrush. 'I might be a bit rusty to start with,' she warned. 'It's been a while since I was in Theatre.'

'We're all having to cope with things being a bit different, but we're managing. It's mostly cleaning up soft-tissue injuries they're sending me at the moment. Some abdominal trauma, too. I think we've got a suspected lacerated liver or spleen next. Right.' Richard used his shoulder to bump open the swing doors into the operating theatre. 'Let's get this show back on the road.'

The first patient was a difficult case. The abdominal bleeding had been slow but steady and by the time the patient had been identified as needing urgent attention, he had already been in hypovolaemic shock. Blood products for transfusion were still in short supply and Richard decided to set up the filtering system that allowed them to give blood suctioned from the abdomen back to the patient. By the time the spleen had been removed and the bleeding controlled, enough blood had been returned to make the anaesthetist a lot happier about the blood pressure he was monitoring.

Sarah was finding it easier to assist than she had expected. The local staff members, including the anaesthetist, Rahjid, knew where to find things, and with both the surgeon and his assistant being in unfamiliar territory they were quite prepared to compromise or scan the trolley themselves for something Sarah was unable to locate.

The next two cases were more stable. An arm wound that hadn't stopped bleeding despite pressure bandaging needed blood vessels tied off. A woman with a horrific slice in her thigh needed deep-tissue irrigation and suturing.

'She looks like she was attacked with a sword,' Sarah commented.

'Sheet of iron blowing from a roof,' Richard told her. 'Same sort of effect in a high wind.'

Sarah found her back aching when she was scrubbing up again for their fourth case. It was nearly six hours since she had arrived at the hospital. Were they due for a break soon or expected to keep working until they dropped?

Kevin was also looking tired. He stretched his back and groaned. 'I'm not used to this. I'm going to need some strong coffee soon.'

'One more case and then we'll all take a break,' Richard promised. 'This patient has just been brought in from one of the outlying islands and it sounds urgent.'

Elena, who had relayed the message, nodded. 'It's a young boy who was washed away in the tidal wave. He got a branch of a tree stabbing into his stomach and his knee was smashed onto rocks.'

'I'll tackle the abdominal wound but that leg injury will need an orthopod.' Richard turned back to Elena. 'Have they finished their case in Theatre 1 yet?'

'Very close, I think. I'll check.'

'Is there an orthopaedic surgeon next door?' Kevin queried. 'That's handy.'

'Not just any orthopaedic surgeon,' Richard responded. 'This guy's a superstar. People travel halfway across the world to get onto his private operating lists. He specialises in paediatric stuff, I believe.'

'He's got a private practice in Fiji?' Kevin's tone reflected Sarah's own astonishment.

'No.' Richard shook his head. 'He's a bit of an unusual case from what I've heard. He's a specialist orthopaedic surgeon most of the time but he spends three months of every year living in the islands and does general orthopaedic surgery and even GP duties while he's here.'

Sarah angled her hands under the running water, rinsing from fingertips to elbows and then changing direction to rinse again from elbows to fingertips. It certainly wasn't the temperature of the water that was causing the goose-bumps that suddenly appeared on her arms.

'Where does he come from?'

'London, I believe.'

Sarah's breath caught as she reached for her towel. 'What's his name?'

'Ben Dawson.'

But it wasn't Richard who spoke. Sarah would have recognised that voice anywhere. She whirled to face the speaker, confusion warring with a far stronger emotion as she saw Ben standing so close. A specialist orthopaedic surgeon? Where did that put any theories about him dropping out from mainstream medical practice?

'Hi, Ben. We're not quite ready for you yet.'

Sarah certainly wasn't ready. She was gaping like a stranded fish, unable to think of anything to say. She could hear an echo of her own words suggesting that Tori needed evacuation because the standard of orthopaedic care in a Pacific island could be considered less than adequate. She tried to smile but her lips were frozen. As locked as her gaze was with that of Ben Dawson.

'This is Sarah, Ben. She's from New Zealand. Just over the ditch from where I come from.'

'Yes.' Ben was frowning. 'Did you have any idea what you were letting yourself in for here, Sarah?'

She shook her head, still mute but finally able to break the eye contact. How could she have known what it would be like to see Ben again? Every cell in her body seemed to have come alive with an energy she had not possessed a minute ago. Ever, in fact. This was so different to meeting Ben the first time.

She had been over every word they had spoken together, every look and touch—so often she felt like she knew this man intimately.

And Tori was right. This was so much more than lust. Sarah could see the lines of weariness etched around Ben's eyes and she wanted to touch them. To try and smooth them away. She wanted to be able to step in and share whatever load was making him look so tired and sad. Her own weariness ceased to have any relevance.

This had nothing to do with attraction.

Was *this* what genuine love felt like?

'I suspect your hands are dry by now.' Probably as dry as Ben's tone, in fact. 'Would you mind if I got near the sink?'

'Of course not.' Sarah moved, thankful that regard for sterility made it necessary to avoid touching as they changed places. A young Fijian nurse was holding a gown ready for her and she plunged her arms into the sleeves and then turned to have it tied. Richard and Kevin had already gone into the theatre.

'How's Victoria?'

Sarah kept her gaze on his hands as they twisted together under the foam from the antiseptic soap.

'She's doing well. In a walking brace, but she wasn't able to volunteer to come on the relief team. She was very disappointed.'

'I'm sure.' The words held about as much sympathy as they had when he'd informed Sarah and Tori that their holiday was over. Maybe he was reminded of that exchange as well. When Sarah glanced up, his eyebrow lifted fractionally. 'It's not going to be much of a holiday this time, you know.'

She made no response to that as she flexed her

fingers, easing the sterile gloves into place. So he *had* been left with the impression that she was only interested in having a good time. That she shared his opinion that if it wasn't fun it wasn't worth bothering with.

At least she had the opportunity to prove him wrong over the next few days, didn't she? Sarah held her hands up, palms facing her, using her back to open the swing doors. Ben Dawson was going to be very impressed with what he saw of Sarah Mitchell from now on. She was going to make sure of that.

Except that it was Sarah who was the one being impressed over the next two hours. Astonishingly impressed.

Ben examined X-rays and then the horrific wound under the dressing. The whole knee looked shattered to Sarah and she wouldn't have been surprised if an amputation had been required, but Ben simply nodded.

'Let's start with some irrigation,' he ordered. 'We'll try and suck out some of the smaller bone fragments. We'll have to do a bit of bone grafting to reconstitute the tibia. We might find some large enough fragments to wire that patella together as well.'

It wasn't just the bones that needed repair. Ligaments, tendons and blood vessels had also been damaged, but Ben appeared unfazed. He worked quickly but meticulously and Sarah had to scramble to find some of the instruments requested. Working with orthopaedic surgeons in the past had been partly why Sarah had left her position as a theatre nurse, but

Ben showed none of the patronising temperament she remembered. Even when she was slow.

'There's a small bone nibbler there—let's have that, thanks, Sarah. Should do the job nicely.'

Richard worked on the abdominal wound, expressing astonishment as he found that the major vessels and organs had all been spared by the puncture wound. He was soon relaxed enough to start chatting to Ben.

'So, you're based in London?'

'Yes. I have a private practice and I do some surgical sessions in quite a few different hospitals.'

'You must be run off your feet. No wonder you want to escape winter every year by coming over here.'

'It's summer at home right now.'

'December wouldn't be a good time over here,' Kevin put in wryly. 'Tropical cyclone season, isn't it?'

Richard reached for the suture Elena was holding out for him and shook his head. 'I forgot you're in the other hemisphere. Must be getting tired.'

'How long have you been operating?'

'Since the last break?' Richard glanced up at the clock. 'Nearly eight hours.'

'You should definitely step down, then. How's the abdomen looking?'

'Astonishingly good. I've left a drain in and we'll need to start antibiotic cover but we're almost closed.'

Dark eyes over the edge of the mask chose another subject to focus on. 'How long have you been on your feet, Sarah?'

'I'm fine,' she responded. She didn't want to be sent away for a rest and replaced by Elena as scrub nurse. 'I'd like to stay.' She wanted to stay. Very much.

After a tiny hesitation, Ben nodded. 'If I have Rahjid looking after the anaesthetic and Sarah scrubbed, we really only need one other nurse as a runner. We've got some fiddly stuff to do with these ligaments but it shouldn't take too long. Elena, how are you holding up?'

'I'm fine, too, Doctor Ben.'

'Go and put your feet up when you've finished closing, then, Richard. You, too, Kevin. Try and get some sleep.'

By the time the theatre emptied of the extra personnel, Ben had finished wiring the larger patella fragments together.

'That's most of it done. We'll just see if we can do a repair of the patella tendon. I'll have some number 1 Vicryl sutures, thanks, Sarah. Let's hope we can protect it without putting any more wire into this knee.'

Sarah took a deep breath. The atmosphere had become almost intimate with the reduction in personnel numbers. Rahjid was quiet, concentrating on his monitors, and Elena was on the other side of the table in the shadows cast by the bright spotlight.

'Why didn't you say anything, Ben?' Sarah asked quietly. 'Why did you let me and Tori assume you were some kind of resort GP?'

Ben shrugged. 'That's what I was at the time.'

'But you specialise in paediatric orthopaedics, right?'

He nodded, talking calmly as he continued working. 'I see all sorts of kids with disease that ends up needing some intervention.'

'What sort of disease?'

'Oh, osteogenesis imperfecta, Marfan syndrome, arthritis, cerebral palsy. There's all sorts. I don't have much to do with osteosarcoma fortunately. Not sure I could handle treating kids with bone cancer. The kind of disabilities my patients have to deal with is stressful enough.'

Any remaining impression of Ben Dawson opting out of a medical career with any significance to play in the sun was wiped out by the depth of involvement Sarah could detect in his words. But it still seemed odd to take so much time off on a regular basis.

'Is that why you come to the islands? To get away from the stress?'

'Partly.' Ben sounded offhand as he concentrated on his ligament reconstruction. 'I actually enjoy doing a bit of general practice. Being a specialist in any field gradually pulls you into a very rigid area. It's nice to get back to grass roots occasionally. Can I have some tissue forceps, please?'

Sarah handed him the instrument but she wasn't convinced. A specialist who was good enough to attract international patients would have a hard job organising three months a year away and still staying on top. Sure, he may earn enough to have been able to purchase an island of his own, and he may well enjoy general practice as a hobby, but there had to be a much better reason than relief from stress to have prompted such a drastically unusual lifestyle. Not only was she unconvinced, Sarah was also very curious.

'Is it orthopaedic surgery you do on your days at the hospitals?'

Ben didn't look up. 'Of course.'

'So it would have been you that repaired Tori's fracture if we'd chosen not to be evacuated.'

'Yes.'

'And you still didn't say anything. You let me spout off about the standard of care being so much less than it would be back in Auckland.' Sarah watched the deft knot tying going on in the tendon repair but refused to be impressed. 'What was that all about?'

'You had me firmly pegged as a resort doctor with a cruisy lifestyle. You'd hardly have leapt at any offer of mine to do the surgery, would you?'

'Probably not,' Sarah admitted. 'All I knew was that you were in a general practitioner role on some islands and that you worked a couple of days a week here at the hospital. That's why I—' Sarah stopped speaking abruptly, horrified at the confession her weariness had been about to lead her into.

'Why you came on the relief team?' Ben's tone had a puzzled frown.

Good grief, did he suspect the ulterior motives that had convinced Sarah to come on this mission? Did she appear to be blatantly chasing him?

'No, of course not,' she said lightly. 'It was just why I chose to come to Suva rather than go to one of the other hospitals. Even a vaguely familiar face in a strange place is nice. I'm feeling way out of my depth here.'

She could see that Ben was smiling beneath his mask by the way the lines deepened around his eyes.

'You're doing just fine, Sarah. I'm glad you chose to come to Suva.'

*   *   *

Was he?

Really?

The startling rush of something akin to pleasure that Ben had experienced on recognising Sarah in the scrub room had been followed by a flash of rather strong annoyance.

Things were quite tough enough right now, without having the complication of the peculiar attraction he'd felt for Sarah Mitchell. One that hadn't been reciprocated, and which had only really begun to fade thanks to the overwhelming demands of the current crisis.

Sarah and her sister had already got themselves into trouble by going somewhere they didn't belong, and after that comment Sarah had made about preferring to be in Suva, Ben couldn't quite shake the suspicion that he figured somewhere on her agenda.

He couldn't deny that she was good to work with, however, and he wouldn't have expected anything less after the initial impression he'd had of her. There was a kind of steadiness about her. A calm that made it deceptively relaxing to be in her company.

Even now, with strident alarm bells ringing, Ben felt inclined to trust her.

No. He blinked hard, trying to persuade tired eyes to focus sharply for a little while longer as he started on the skin sutures this wound needed. Trust was dangerous. He might find himself actually prepared to forgive her, and risk further rejection of an interest he should never have revealed in the first place.

It would be a relief to finish this surgery. He should have sent Sarah away to rest when Richard and Kevin had gone. He was too aware of her standing so close. He could even smell a faint scent of her—an occasional waft of something fresh like a fruit-flavoured shampoo that cut through the clinical smell of the operating theatre.

He could sense every tiny movement she made and when their hands touched, as they did now with the passing of a fresh suture needle and thread, Ben could feel the astonishing tingle of her skin even through the gloves.

Or was it just his skin that tingled?

He was too tired, dammit. He didn't need this. Didn't want it.

It was a huge relief to finish the surgery and hand their young patient over to the staff from the recovery area.

'Elena will show you where to go for your break,' he told Sarah. 'Thanks for your help.'

He watched as she pulled her gloves and mask off to throw them away. Seeing her whole face again was almost a shock. So was the way that long braid of dark hair fell down her back when her theatre cap was removed. Would he even see Sarah again? She would be sent home in a day or two when the situation was under better control, and for the rest of her time here she could well be put into a ward or another theatre or in with a crowd in the emergency department. He might never see her again.

Ben didn't want that.

'Do you know where you'll be used next?' he queried.

Sarah was rubbing the back of her neck. 'No. I'm assuming it'll be in Theatre again. Maybe I'll see you later.'

'Maybe.' Ben hesitated but *maybe* just wasn't good enough. 'I'm heading off to find Dr Singh to see where I'm most needed. Do you want to come with me?'

She seemed to be considering the option rather carefully, but when she smiled the air around Ben felt suddenly warmer.

'Yes,' she said, still smiling. 'Thanks, Ben. I'd like that.'

CHAPTER SEVEN

'BEN! Just the man I need.'

Dr Singh was moving at speed to intercept Ben and Sarah well before they reached his office. 'We've got a boat available and things have calmed down enough to send a small team out to check on some of the islands that have been cut off. We're particularly concerned about Matalevu Island. It's got one of the biggest populations and was directly in the path of the storm. You know these villages better than anyone else I could find. Could you do it?'

'Sure.'

Visibly relieved, Dr Singh glanced at Sarah and smiled somewhat distractedly. 'Hello. You're one of the Australian team, aren't you?'

'New Zealand. We arrived about eight or nine hours ago.'

'How are you holding up?'

Sarah wasn't about to admit to fatigue or shock when Ben had just agreed to carry on without any detectable hesitation. 'I'm fine.'

'You a doctor?'

'No, just a nurse.'

'No 'just' about it,' Ben put in. 'Sarah's been assisting me in some rather delicate surgery. She's extremely competent.'

The brief glance he gave Sarah was warm enough to add considerably to the effect of the approbation.

'Ah, yes—I remember you now. You went early

from the briefing to help out in Theatre 2.' Dr Singh's glance travelled from Sarah back to Ben. 'You're going to need some assistance with this mission.'

'I think Sarah is overdue for a break.'

'I'm fine,' Sarah insisted.

'Are you sure?'

Ben was frowning but Sarah met the searching gaze calmly. 'I'm sure,' she affirmed quietly. The prospect of working with Ben away from the hospital seemed to have been snatched from one of the fantasies that call-up telephone conversation had induced. She wasn't about to let it slip through her fingers.

Dr Singh was nodding as though the arrangement was satisfactorily confirmed. 'We still need another doctor to go, though.'

'Kevin's had a bit of a break. I could ask him.'

'Kevin?'

Sarah nodded. She almost smiled. If it wasn't completely within the realms of fantasy, she could have imagined Ben's tone to convey something more than doubt. Jealousy even?

'Who's Kevin?' Dr Singh asked.

'He's a surgical registrar from New Zealand. He went with me to help in Theatre 2.'

'Ah, yes. So he did.' Dr Singh shook his head. 'I could be losing the plot here.'

Ben smiled. 'I doubt that.'

Dr Singh didn't see the smile, because he was still focussed on Sarah. 'If he's happy to go, that's great. See if you can find him, would you, Sarah? If that's all right with you, Ben?' he added hurriedly.

Ben's smile faded. 'It's fine with me. How soon will we leave?'

'I've got an ED nurse putting together supplies for

you and there's a van waiting to take you to the wharf. Thirty minutes?'

Ben's nod was terse. 'Find yourself something to eat, Sarah. I'll meet you outside.'

'Woo-*hoo*!' Kevin had a huge grin on his face as the jet boat left the crest of a swell and was airborne momentarily before crashing into the lower slopes of the next swell. 'I wasn't expecting excitement like this!'

Sarah just shook her head. She was hanging on for dear life in the rough sea and feeling very thankful for the lifejacket she was wearing. The small cabin of the boat was filled with supplies and she and Kevin were using the two seats near the engine. Ben stood beside the boat's pilot, one hand on the rail above the wheel, the other shading his eyes against the intermittent brightness of sunshine finally breaking through the cloud cover.

It was inevitable that she'd be reminded of the last boat trip she had shared with Ben, but Sarah found the humiliation and disappointment she remembered so well was gone. Anxiety was still present but this time it wasn't centred on a close family member. Sarah could feel empathy for the injured they were going to find and treat but, if she was honest with herself, her anxiety was more to do with what Ben might think of her performance.

He would expect a lot, if the people he worked with had to meet his own standards of performance. This wasn't the first time Sarah had been aware of the commanding presence he had in an emergency. He had been completely professional and efficient in his treatment of Tori that day. There was something very,

very solid about this man and having to let go of at least one of her assumptions about his lightweight career and social ambitions left her feeling as though she had misjudged him badly.

It was also scary. Maybe she had known instinctively right from the start that Ben Dawson was trustworthy. The powerful physical attraction might, in fact, be secondary to something that was far more important. And elusive.

Sarah had never trusted any man enough to give herself heart and soul to a relationship. She was quite old enough and wise enough now to know it was unlikely she would meet someone else who had the kind of qualities she strongly suspected Ben to possess.

What if Ben felt absolutely nothing for her in return? She would have come here, discovered the truth about how she felt about him and why, and then she would then have to go home—alone—with the knowledge that she was unlikely to ever find such an opportunity again.

This was *it*, as Tori would say.

Sarah didn't want to lose it.

There was some hope, wasn't there? He couldn't have kissed her the way he had if he'd felt nothing, surely. He could have objected to being sent out in such a small team with her to assist him if he didn't want her near. He wasn't angry, as he had been on that last boat trip. He looked just as serious but they were on the same side now, weren't they? Almost—

'Bit scary, huh?' Ben had turned and caught Sarah's stare.

She nodded but managed to smile. Thank goodness he didn't know what she was *really* so scared of!

'Won't be much longer,' Ben shouted. 'You're quite safe, Sarah. There won't be any sharks around in this weather.'

Once inside the protection of the island's coral reef, the sea was relatively calm. The sun appeared for long enough to give the water some of the turquoise colouring Sarah remembered so well and for its heat to feel familiar, but there was no feeling of setting foot in paradise this time.

Palm trees had been stripped of fruit and leaves and some even uprooted. The white sand of the beach was littered with debris from bures that had been unable to stand up to the storm. Buildings further inland had been a little more protected but the damage was widespread. Crops had been flattened and dead goats and pigs were an indication that livestock had fared little better.

There were still smiling children to meet the arrivals, however, and adults to carry the supplies. Cries of 'Doctor Ben' echoed as some ran ahead to tell others. Sarah and Kevin found their hands being held by small guides, but Sarah was distracted by a small girl who couldn't keep up with the others.

Some kind of foot deformity had her limping badly enough to be left behind and, having turned her head more than once to monitor her progress, Sarah finally stopped, eased her hands free from her guides' and went back to pick up the child. Maybe it was the memory of Ben scooping up that small girl overcome with shyness that prompted the quick cuddle and kiss on a cheek before hurrying to catch up with the group.

More adults came to greet them, the relief in their expressions suggesting that the team's skills would be needed, and Sarah put the little girl back on her feet as they neared the hub of the village. Ambulatory patients began to gather but for some time Ben, Kevin and Sarah were too busy inside the village church that had been turned into a makeshift medical centre.

Several people lay on mattresses and two of them were seriously injured enough to need urgent evacuation. One had a depressed skull fracture, having been hit by a piece of timber. The other had been crushed by a falling tree and clearly had fractured ribs and abdominal trauma. They both had other, less serious injuries, with lacerations and bruising.

For some time the atmosphere was tense as the team worked to stabilise these two well enough for transport. IV lines were put in and fluids given to try and raise blood pressure to an acceptable level. Oxygen and pain relief were administered. Open wounds were dressed and recordings of all vital signs made and monitored.

The woman with the skull fracture was unconscious and needed airway protection before transport. It was Ben who performed the intubation, with Sarah assisting. The respiratory distress of the man with the fractured ribs was a worry but his deteriorating condition due to the internal blood loss was of even more concern. Even after running in two litres of saline, the systolic blood pressure barely reached an acceptable level.

'He needs an urgent laparotomy,' Ben decided. 'Both these patients need to be on that boat—now. And they need an escort.'

'We've got at least two fractured femurs and some more abdo and chest injuries in here.' Kevin looked around at the other patients in the church. 'And have you seen how many people are waiting outside? You could spend all day just suturing lacerations.'

'I'll get on with dealing with these patients,' Ben said. 'I'd like you to escort the first lot back to hospital, Kevin.'

'By myself?'

Ben nodded. 'You should be able to do the whole circuit within a couple of hours. Sarah and I will have triaged everybody else by then, I hope. At least we'll have a good idea of how many more people will need evacuation.'

'Do you want any more supplies brought back?'

'Yes. More antibiotics. And dressings.'

'Anything personal? Clothes or food maybe?'

'They'll look after us here. The women are starting to prepare a meal already, but we'll wait until you get back to take a break.'

It was nearly three hours before the boat returned with Kevin and the time of working one on one with Ben had been a revelation to Sarah.

If Sarah had written a list of things she wanted to find out about the man she thought she was in love with, she couldn't have come up with a better way of ticking the items off.

She could see his warmth in the way he greeted and reassured people. His gentleness in the way he examined them. She saw compassion when one of the women needing attention turned out to be the wife of the village's only fatality, and Ben held the sobbing woman in his arms for a minute before even asking about her physical injuries.

His strength was astounding and Sarah found she was drawing on it more and more as her own physical weariness made it harder to function. Every smile or word of praise kept her going just a little longer and Ben clearly knew just when she needed it.

'You're doing well, Sarah. Keep it up.

'I like that splinting job you've done. The capillary refill is much better.'

He was human, himself, of course, and at one point Sarah went outside and found him leaning against the wall, his eyes closed, looking totally exhausted. For an instant Sarah could see a vulnerability in his face that made her catch her breath. The desire to protect—and cherish—this man was overwhelming. And when he opened his eyes a second later, caught her gaze and smiled softly, she was completely undone.

No matter how he felt about her, there would be no escaping the love Sarah felt for Ben. Not ever. The realisation was so huge Sarah found it too difficult to return the smile. Instead, she looked away and took refuge in changing more than the direction of her gaze. The subject was easy to choose.

'Have you seen that little girl over there? The one that limps?'

'Mmm.' Ben sounded as weary as he looked. 'Talipes calcaneovalgus. She seems to cope rather well, though.'

'Talipes? Isn't that clubfoot?'

'Yes, but this variety is dorsiflexed and everted. The underlying structural abnormality is less profound than a fixed clubfoot. If it had been treated at birth it could have been corrected without surgery.'

'Could it still be corrected now?'

Ben smiled. 'I'll have a word with her mother if I get the chance and suggest that she comes to see me some time. I think we've got enough to do right now, though, don't you?'

Sarah had to agree. 'I'm a bit worried about the man with the broken ankle and femur. Asa, isn't it? He doesn't understand me but I'm sure his level of consciousness has dropped a bit. He's very drowsy and rather clammy. His BP's fallen since last time, though the systolic is still 110. I'm just wondering if the blood loss from his fractures has been enough to put him into shock or whether we might have missed some other injury.'

'Let's go and check.

'I think you're right,' Ben said a short time later. 'He's got abdominal discomfort that he didn't have earlier. Or maybe the pain from the broken femur was overriding it. Let's get another IV and some more fluids into him. We'll also put him at the top of the list for the next evacuation boat.'

Kevin arrived back as daylight began to fade so there was no time to waste. The seas were still not quiet enough to risk transferring patients in the dark. With another two on stretchers gone and two more ambulatory patients using the seats in the boat, Ben and Sarah remained on the island.

The urgency had dissipated but there were still plenty of people needing treatment for more minor injuries.

'We'll have something to eat and then work for as long as we can tonight,' Ben decided. 'We should be able to get a few hours' sleep before they come back for us at dawn.' He spoke to the islanders still waiting patiently to see him and then turned back to Sarah. 'They're happy to wait. Can you check on the ones inside? I've got a couple of phone calls I really need to make.'

'Sure.' Sarah watched him walk away in the direction of the beach as she went back inside the small church. Obviously the calls were of a private nature and something like panic poked an icy finger towards her heart. Was he calling his wife?

Who had been inside his house that day and why hadn't she wanted to answer the door?

Twenty minutes later several of the village women came to fetch Sarah. With broken English and sign language, they indicated that they would be taking care of the injured while she went to have a meal.

'Where Doctor Ben?' one asked.

Sarah mimed talking on a telephone and pointed towards the beach, but that caused only tilted heads and uncomprehending expressions.

'I'll find him,' she promised.

It wasn't difficult. When Sarah reached the beach and saw the discarded clothing beside the satellite phone, she quickly spotted Ben swimming in the lagoon as splashing water caught and magnified the pale moonlight. Without hesitation, Sarah pulled her own clothes off, apart from her underwear. What better way could there be to wash away the grime and weariness of such a long day? Someone would come and find them if there was a problem with any of the remaining patients, and being a few minutes later to eat their meal shouldn't offend anybody.

The water felt as glorious as Sarah had anticipated and the release of tension through physical exertion gave her an almost euphoric sensation. When she saw that she had caught up with Ben, she actually laughed aloud.

'This is wonderful. I wouldn't have thought of it if I hadn't seen you out here. I love swimming at night and some exercise is just what I needed.'

'Race you to the other side, then.'

The distance was not much more than a hundred metres but it was far enough for Sarah to show off the pace that had won more than a few competitions in her teens. It was more of an effort than she'd expected to keep up with Ben, however, and Sarah had to concede defeat when she saw him treading water and waiting for her as they neared the edge of the lagoon.

'Hey, you can swim!' Sarah exclaimed.

'So can you.'

Suddenly shy under Ben's gaze, Sarah blinked the salt water from her eyes. 'I was supposed to come and tell you that dinner was ready.'

'Great. I'm starving.'

'Me, too. We've worked pretty hard today, haven't we?'

'Sure have.' Ben's gaze held something very like respect. 'You've been fantastic, Sarah. Thank you.'

'Glad to help.'

'We'd better head back to shore.'

Sarah nodded but waited for Ben to start swimming again. When he rolled onto his back and drifted lazily for a moment, she took a deep breath.

'I was hoping I might see you over here, Ben.'

'Oh?' He sounded wary.

'I wanted a chance to apologise. For...for trespassing on your island that day.'

'Forget it. It didn't matter.' Ben twisted with a dolphin-like movement and struck off in a slow breast-stroke towards the shore.

Sarah followed. The casual dismissal of her apology wasn't enough. 'It seemed to,' she said. 'You were very angry.'

'That wasn't what I was angry about.'

Sarah swam a few more strokes. 'What were you angry about?'

The silence lasted another few strokes.

'Ben?'

'You really want to know?'

'Yes.'

Ben stopped swimming and stood up in the chest-deep water. He stared at Sarah for a moment and then shook his head. 'I was angry about Tori.'

'So you knew it was her idea to find your island?'

'No.'

'Because she broke her leg? It was hardly intentional.'

'No. Not because she broke her leg.'

Sarah hesitated. She had the opportunity to explore some far more personal ground but was she brave enough to try? 'Be-because she found you attractive?'

Ben was avoiding her gaze. His voice sounded strained. Accusatory. 'No. It was because I found *you* attractive.'

'Oh…' This was what she had wanted to hear, wasn't it? So why did she feel so terrified?

'I *kissed* you.' Ben sounded almost surprised now. 'And it was something rather special. The only thing you had to say about it was that it should have been Tori I was kissing.' His breath came out in a huff of unamused laughter. 'You turn up at my home and I thought maybe you had felt the same way about that kiss after all, but you open your mouth and practically your first word is "Tori". "Tori needs you", you said. You were so determined to hand me on. Like a discarded *toy* or something.' Now that he had started talking, the words just kept rushing out. 'You weren't interested but Tori was. What I thought didn't count for anything, did it?'

'That's not true.'

'How can you deny what you said? I remember every word.'

'I know what I said. I remember it, too. But it's still not all true.'

'Which bit isn't?'

'The bit about me not being interested. I *was*, but…'

'But?'

'But Tori saw you first.'

Even in the dark, the look Sarah received made her cringe. The water was beginning to feel cold as well and she shivered.

'OK. The truth is that I didn't see the point of some holiday fling. That was all you would have wanted. You said yourself, "If it isn't fun it's not worth bothering with". I'm not going to sleep with someone I'm not in love with and I don't believe in love at first sight.'

'Neither do I.'

Another silence stretched between them. And then…

'At least, I never used to.' Ben sighed softly. 'Something weird happened, though. I haven't been able to forget you.'

Sarah swallowed hard. 'Same,' she murmured.

'I couldn't believe it when I walked into that scrub room and saw you. I thought I was hallucinating from exhaustion or something.'

Ben's hands felt rough as he took hold of her upper arms. '*Why* did you come back, Sarah?'

'Because they asked me. And because…I wanted to see you again.'

The pull on her arms unbalanced Sarah and her whole body floated to meet Ben's as he drew their faces close enough for their lips to touch. Then his arms steadied her, sliding down her back to hold her against him, and she reached out to wrap her arms around his neck, conscious of nothing other than the need to prolong the kiss.

It was the same as the first time. Electric. Compelling. Overwhelming. But it was different as well. There was a hunger that had only been hinted at previously. A need to go further. This wasn't an isolated experience. It was just a beginning.

Tori had been so right. Sarah had never been *really* in love before. She had been attracted enough to think she was on the right track. 'In love' enough to have a physical relationship, even fond enough of her partner to think it could work long term. But it never had and now she had more than an inkling why.

This was so different. Sexual feelings were underpinned with other desires. The caring. The instinct to protect and comfort. The desire to share things she had never shared—with anyone.

And his touch made her lose herself. To enter a realm of sensation and closeness that drew her compellingly forward towards something she had never believed really existed. Was it a connection of the soul as well as the body?

Was it a journey she would dare to take?

With Ben…yes. She couldn't hold back. As his hand pushed her bra up to free her breasts to his touch, Sarah found herself arching towards him, her hands holding his head so that she didn't lose the contact with his lips.

The shouting from the shore was the only thing that could have made them pull apart. The moon had been obscured by cloud but the cover of darkness was no excuse to ignore the call. Someone might need their medical skills.

Ben shouted something in Fijian. 'We'd better go back,' he told Sarah. 'They're worried about us.' His lips touched hers again, more gently this time. 'We'll continue this discussion later.'

'Mmm.' Sarah swam alongside Ben into the shallows. 'I hope so.'

Except they never got the opportunity. Halfway through a simple meal of fish and sweet potato, Ben's phone rang.

'What?' Sarah could hear the anxiety in his voice. 'How did that happen? How much pain is she in?' He listened for a moment. 'I'm on my way,' he said firmly. 'I'll meet you at the hospital.'

'Complications with a patient?' Sarah asked.

'No. It's…' Ben gave her a very peculiar look. The shake of his head made it seem as though he'd decided against telling her something. 'I have to get back to the mainland. You'll need to stay here, Sarah, if that's all right. Keep an eye on things. Dress any wounds that still need attention. The suturing will just have to wait a little longer. They'll send a boat in the morning to get you and any other patients that need to be transferred.'

She had no choice. The only boat available to take Ben back to the mainland was tiny, and they couldn't leave the islanders without any medical care for the rest of the night.

'Will I see you again?' Sarah felt completely shut out as preparations were made and Ben made his way to the island's wharf. She felt as though the discussion and kiss in the lagoon had never happened.

'Of course.' But Ben was clearly distracted. He was thinking of someone other than her right now. 'I'll come and find you tomorrow.'

'I don't know where I'll be.'

'Don't worry.' For a split second, Sarah seemed to be in his focus again and she could see her own longing mirrored in Ben's dark eyes. 'I'll find you.'

CHAPTER EIGHT

THE coffee was stone cold.

Ben tipped the remaining contents of the mug into the sink, wondering how the last fifteen minutes had evaporated so quickly. He was due back in Theatre and yet another opportunity to look for Sarah or at least enquire as to her whereabouts had been lost.

It was mid-afternoon now. She would have been brought back from the outlying island this morning. He'd hoped she would be working in Theatre again but she hadn't appeared.

And maybe that was for the best.

The desire to see her again, to *touch* her, was fierce enough to be a warning in itself. This wasn't the kind of attraction that could satisfy briefly and then be put aside, and that was the only kind of satisfaction that had been on his agenda for the last few years. The only kind he could afford to allow himself.

The single time he had risked more had been a disaster. The rejection had been far more hurtful because it hadn't been his own attractions that had been deemed unacceptable. To have what mattered more than himself rejected so completely had given birth to the vow that Ben would never trust a woman to that extent again.

But Sarah Mitchell was different, wasn't she?

Seeing her make the effort to include that little girl with the clubfoot yesterday—to offer both acceptance and genuine affection—had snapped something rather painful deep within his heart. The expression on her face when she had pointed out the child later and asked if the deformity could still be corrected had touched the spot where that pain had been, and to Ben's astonishment he'd discovered it didn't hurt any more.

Yes. Sarah was different. But he'd known that from the first moment he'd seen her, hadn't he? She had the potential to disrupt a life he'd spent years shaping into something he could cope with. He was not about to risk having to go through that process again. He *couldn't*.

They had practically admitted they were in love with each other. Another step and there would be no going back. Even if he was prepared to take the risk on his own behalf, he didn't have the right to inflict the possible fallout on anyone else. Especially on—

'Doctor Ben? Are you ready?'

'Coming, Elena.' Ben didn't even cast a glance around the corridor as he made his way back to Theatre 1. It might be painful but it was better to be this way.

He'd coped with painful things before. This feeling of devastation wouldn't last.

He hadn't come to find her.

Sarah had officially finished the duty she had been assigned in the paediatric ward on her return from Matalevu island this morning, but she was still here, reluctant to go and find her temporary accommodation or fellow team members. There was talk of sending the medical relief team home the next day.

With a steady stream of evacuation of the more seriously injured over the last two days and the number of new patients presenting themselves returning to normal levels, the crisis was on the way to being resolved. Wards were the areas under pressure now as the injured convalesced.

The operating theatres were still busy with surgery for less life-threatening injuries, and Sarah wasn't sure why she had chosen to help in the wards instead. Perhaps she didn't want to look desperate by flinging herself in Ben's path again. Maybe it was that she needed to know whether the signals she had received from Ben last night had been genuine.

If they were, he would come and find her.

But he hadn't come and soon Sarah would be having a meal in the company of other volunteer medical staff. And sleeping, hopefully. Despite several hours of deep sleep on the island last night, Sarah was exhausted, and that was probably the real reason she had chosen to work in the familiar area of a children's ward.

It didn't matter that she didn't speak their language. The nursing staff spoke English quite well enough to let her know what was needed and children were the same, no matter what their nationality. They all needed care with medicine and dressings, food, clothes, bathing and clean nappies. The same things made them laugh. Or cry. They all responded to a smile or a cuddle.

Most of the patients had a mother or grandmother there and some had siblings adding to the colour and noise. The playroom was well stocked with toys and many children were well enough for discharge, having been kept in for observation after a minor head injury or while waiting for a cast to dry.

Sarah had been assigned to a room with more seriously injured young patients. One had needed surgery to remove a ruptured spleen, an older child was being kept immobilised with a lumbar spine injury and another had broken both legs and several ribs, which made breathing too uncomfortable without pain relief.

Also in the room was the little boy Ben had operated on yesterday, and Sarah had spent a lot of time with him that afternoon. A dressing change on his abdominal wound had just been completed and Sarah took the contaminated dressing to the sluice room to put into the bag destined for incineration.

Dr Dawson hadn't been to check on this patient today but the Australian surgeon, Richard, had come in briefly. Having checked his own work on the abdominal injury, he took a moment to admire the reconstruction of the boy's knee.

'Would you look at that? I wouldn't have thought it was possible to put that lot back together so neatly. He's something else, that Ben Dawson.'

'Sure is.' Sarah kept her tone carefully neutral. 'Have you been working with him today?'

'No such luck. He was tied up in Theatre 1 all morning and I think he might have gone for the day now. I couldn't find him when I went to say goodbye. I'm heading home with my family tonight.'

'They don't need you any more?'

'I'm sure they'll be happy to take any assistance they're offered, but I feel like I've done my bit and the worst seems to be over. How long are you going to stay, Sarah?'

'I don't know. I'll stay as long as I'm wanted, I guess.'

Wanted by *whom*? Sarah asked herself as she left

the sluice room. The hospital administration or Ben Dawson?

The door just ahead of her had been closed when she'd walked past a minute ago. It was open just an inch or two now and Sarah could see what appeared to be an eye watching her. Effectively distracted from another session of thinking about Ben and ending up feeling bewildered and hurt, Sarah paused and smiled. Then she crouched to be on the same level as the eye.

'Hello,' she whispered. 'I can see you.'

The giggle was a surprise. Did the eye's owner understand English?

'I'm Sarah,' she told the eye. 'What's your name?'

The door opened another inch and Sarah's heart skipped a beat as the small scarred face came into view.

'You're Phoebe!' she exclaimed. She looked over the child's shoulder expecting to see the nanny, but the tiny room was empty apart from a single bed and a chair. The bed had several toys and books on it and among the pile of treasures was something that made Sarah smile again.

'You still have your pretty shell!'

Phoebe nodded but eyed Sarah a little warily. 'Phoebe's shell,' she said firmly.

'Of course it is,' Sarah agreed. 'I'm just glad you still like it.'

The tiny girl was still half hiding behind the door. 'Are you all right, sweetheart?' Sarah asked. 'Are you here because you're sick?'

'No. I hurted my arm. On some glass that broke in the wind.' The door opened further and Phoebe displayed a bandage that covered her arm from wrist to elbow. 'I got sewed up.'

'Did you, darling? Did it hurt?'

Phoebe shook her head. 'I was asleep. Then I got a lollipop.'

Sarah took another glance into the room she hadn't even realised contained a patient. Why was Phoebe in here if she'd only been in to have a laceration sutured? And why was she alone?

'Are you all by yourself, Phoebe?'

She nodded. 'Nanny's gone to get more close for me. I'm going home soon.'

'That's good.' Sarah still wasn't happy to leave such a young child alone to wait. 'Do you want to come and play with the other children until Nanny comes back?'

A curious mix of eagerness and anxiety in Phoebe's expression made Sarah hesitate. Surely Phoebe was still too young to be shy because of her disfigurement? Sarah held out her hand. 'I could come with you, if you like.'

The nod was quite definite this time. So was the grip of the small hand that slipped into Sarah's.

'Phoebe play.'

Sarah played, too. She was officially off duty after all, and if the nursing staff needed help with a crisis they would come and find her. There were almost a dozen children of varying ages in the playroom. Probably siblings of patients, Sarah decided, as they all looked healthy and there were no adults there to supervise them.

The play was congenial, with a few children of about seven or eight years old building a construction with wooden blocks. Toy cars were being pushed around with accompanying noises by another, and a doll was being stripped carefully by a curious small boy. Activity ceased for a moment when Sarah and Phoebe entered the room and they received equally curious stares.

'*Bula*,' Sarah greeted the children. She smiled and then squeezed Phoebe's hand encouragingly. 'Let's see what we can find to play with, sweetheart. Oh, look! What's that?'

'That' turned out to be an old hand puppet. A once white dog with floppy black ears. Sarah picked it up while Phoebe stood staring as the other children went back to their own games. She put the puppet on her hand. She made it hide below her arm and then pop over the top.

'Woof!'

Phoebe looked as startled as the younger child sitting nearby, who had been busily sucking a cloth book. Sarah made the puppet hide behind her back this time and then reappear.

'*Woof!*'

The toddler's face split into a huge grin and Phoebe giggled.

'Do it again,' she commanded.

So Sarah sat on the old armchair in the corner of the room. She used a cushion as a wall and made the puppet sniff its way along the edge and then fall off.

'Oops!'

This time her efforts were greeted by laughter and the children pushing toy cars abandoned their race. Sarah was offered another old puppet from the toy box, a lion this time. The dog saw the lion and got a terrible fright. It got chased by the lion all around the armchair. It hid and kept popping up but the lion was always looking the wrong way.

By now Sarah had the avid attention of every child

in the room, and the shrieks of laughter were getting steadily louder. One of the nursing staff came to see what was happening and ended up sitting on the floor with Phoebe and the toddler in her lap, laughing as hard as the rest of Sarah's audience.

With the lion about to pounce on the unsuspecting dog and the children all shouting a warning, Sarah happened to glance up to find more adults crowding the doorway, and suddenly her performance died.

Ben had come to find her after all, but he was staring at her as though she had beamed in from some alien planet. The Fijian woman beside him looked like Chicken Little after the sky had fallen.

It took a second for the children to realise why the show had been interrupted. Then Phoebe scrambled off the nurse's lap and let go of the other child's hand.

'Nanny! Have you got my new close?'

The nurse on the floor clearly thought she should appear as if she was there on a mission, and she clapped her hands and issued orders that started the older children tidying toys away. Sarah pulled the puppets from her hands, too embarrassed to look at the doorway again. How long had Ben being watching her act like a complete fool?

The nurse picked up the toddler and left the room, with several more children following. Phoebe had already gone and there was no reason for Sarah to delay her departure any longer. She stood up slowly and moved, but her exit through the doorway was blocked.

By Ben.

'What did you think you were doing, Sarah?'

The disapproving frown on his face was the last expression Sarah would have hoped to see. Or expected, for that matter. What was so wrong with what she had been doing? OK, the show had been a bit silly. With the language barrier, Sarah had had to make do with just sounds and exaggerated gestures and facial expressions, but the children had loved it.

'I'm off duty,' she said a little defensively. 'I was just clowning around. Is that a problem?'

'Who gave you permission to take Phoebe out of her room?'

'Ah...' Sarah's thoughts whirled. Had Phoebe needed orthopaedic care of some kind due to her severe burns? Was she a longstanding patient of Ben's? Maybe there was a reason she had been in isolation. A risk of infection or something. Sarah swallowed. 'No one,' she admitted slowly. 'But she was all by herself. She said she was waiting for her nanny to come back.'

'And it was your idea to drag her in here?'

'I didn't *drag* her.' Sarah pushed back the memory of that momentary hesitation on Phoebe's part. 'I thought she might be lonely with no one to play with.'

'Did it not occur to you to check whether there was a reason she was in a private room?' Ben's tone was enough to make the last of the children stare. Then they edged past the adults and left the room.

'She said she'd been in to have a laceration on her arm sutured. She certainly didn't look as though she was suffering from any contagious disease.' Sarah frowned. 'Why *is* she in a private room?'

'Because her parents requested it.'

'What? Why on earth would they do that?'

The hostility in Ben's gaze sent a chill down Sarah's spine. She had been convinced, only yesterday, of this man's compassion and his rapport with children. It was a big part of what she loved about him. Had she been completely wrong in her character analysis? If so, she needed to find out. It was simply unbelievable that he could actually support Phoebe's exclusion from contact with other children.

'Because she looks a bit different?' Sarah shook her head dismissively. 'That's bizarre. Children don't practise that kind of prejudice. Not at Phoebe's age anyway. Keeping her isolated is the worst thing they could do.'

'And you're an expert? On the strength of, what— two or three years as a paediatric nurse?'

Where on earth was this coming from? Sarah stared back at Ben, refusing to be intimidated.

'I think I've had enough experience to trust my instincts. Children need to feel accepted, Ben, even if they *do* look a bit different. What about that little girl with the clubfoot yesterday? Sure, she had trouble keeping up with the others but she didn't want to be left out, did she?'

'What is it with you and disabled children, Sarah?'

'What do you mean?'

'You seem to home in on them. Pick them out for attention. Don't you think *that* might make them feel different?'

'I...'

Did it? Sarah had never considered that possibility. She had always simply followed her heart.

'They don't need people who make a show of feeling sorry for them. They're people, not stray pets.'

Sarah was stung. This felt like a personal attack now. She straightened her spine. 'Maybe,' she said coldly, 'I understand what it feels like to be a bit different. I know it's easier to hide but it's a huge mistake in the long run. Sure, someone like Phoebe is going to come across rejection but she'll also find love that *doesn't* come from pity.' Sarah wasn't going to be the first to break eye contact, no matter how hard it was to maintain. 'If she isn't hidden away, she might learn that the people who really count are the ones that can see past what's on the surface. Past the scars,' she finished more quietly.

There was a second of silence. And then another. Sarah chewed the inside of her lip. 'I'd be interested to talk to Phoebe's parents,' she added calmly. 'If she has any that actually give a damn.'

'What the hell is that supposed to mean?'

'Well, I've met her twice now and she's only had a nanny for company.'

'Twice?'

'She was in the emergency department that day I was waiting for Tori. I gave her one of the shells I had.'

'You gave her that shell?'

Sarah nodded.

'And told her she was pretty?'

'She is. The side of her face that isn't scarred was what I saw first. She's a beautiful child.'

Ben looked away. 'You have no right to interfere.'

'I'm not *trying* to interfere! For heaven's sake, Ben, what is the problem? And why are you so bothered? If Phoebe's parents are upset, I'm more than happy to talk to them.'

'You are.'

'Sorry?' Ben's terse response had been a statement, not a request for clarification.

'Phoebe only has one parent. And you are.'

'I am what?'

'Talking to him.' Ben's gaze met Sarah's again and it felt like a physical blow. 'I'm Phoebe's father.'

Sarah sucked in a breath. Suddenly things fell into place. The anxious expression on the nanny's face. The door to his house being virtually slammed in her face. 'And you keep her shut away? How could you *do* that, Ben?'

'I know what's best for my daughter. Maybe I don't want her to be the subject of ridicule…or disgust.'

'You mean *you* don't want to be.'

'I beg your pardon?'

'Phoebe's a little girl. How old is she—three?'

'Just turned four.'

'And you've kept her isolated? It's you that's felt the hurt of people's reactions, Ben, not Phoebe. Is that why you come to the islands? To shut both of you away?'

'That's none of your business.'

'No,' Sarah agreed. 'And I don't want it to be. You're not the man I thought you were, Ben Dawson.'

'I'm sorry to disappoint you.' Ben looked as upset as Sarah was feeling. 'But it needn't be a problem for long. Our return to London was delayed by this cyclone. Things are under better control now so we'll be leaving the islands tomorrow.'

'But you can't do that!'

Ben raised an eyebrow, clearly astonished by Sarah's vehemence.

'You've got patients who still need you,' Sarah exclaimed. 'That little boy with the shattered knee isn't out of the woods yet. And how many people are still waiting with complicated fractures that need attention? What about that little girl with the clubfoot?'

'They'll be attended to.'

'By someone with your level of expertise?'

Ben shrugged. 'I can't help everybody. I have my own life to consider and my daughter has to take priority again now.'

'Of course,' Sarah said tightly. 'Heavens, she's been exposed to a roomful of laughing children. It must be time to whisk her back into solitude again.'

'Don't judge what you don't know anything about, Sarah.'

'Does your housekeeper or nanny have permanent instructions to shut the door of your house in the face of any visitors? Did you buy a whole *island* just to shut yourselves away?'

Ben said nothing as he turned towards the door.

'Is Phoebe always shut into a private room or cubicle in the emergency department if she comes into hospital for treatment?'

Ben was disappearing through the doorway now.

'Who's really got the disability, Ben?' Sarah didn't raise her voice. Her words were really only intended for herself. 'Phoebe…or *you*?'

CHAPTER NINE

'DON'T even *think* about it, Sas.'

'Why not?'

'Because coming home now is the *worst* thing you could do.'

'He hates me, Tori.' Sarah glanced around but she was still alone in the pocket of hospital gardens where she had found good reception for her cellphone. 'He thinks I latch onto handicapped children because I feel sorry for them.'

'Well, you do,' Tori said calmly. 'But it's not as though it's just physical deformity that attracts you.'

'You make me sound like some kind of freak. That's exactly what Ben seems to think.'

'Oh, rot. He just doesn't know how much you love kids in general. He also doesn't know that *you* know what it's like to feel unwanted. You should tell him.'

'Fat chance of that. He's gone. Back to his island hide-away with Phoebe. And they're going back to London tomorrow, remember?'

'You really think he's going to leave while they still need him?'

Sarah closed her eyes for a moment to listen to her instincts instead of the confusing jangle of thoughts that had been bombarding her for the last few hours.

'No,' she said eventually. 'If he's really the kind of person I think he is, he won't go home just yet.'

'Then neither should you.'

'But there's a plane leaving first thing in the morning and I've been offered a seat.'

'They also said they'd be happy to have you stay for a few days longer, didn't they?'

'They don't really need me any more and I don't see how staying would help as far as Ben's concerned. We didn't exactly part on friendly terms and I still don't agree with the way he's treating Phoebe.'

'He's trying to protect her. Maybe there's a reason for it. Maybe she's been badly treated in the past.' Sarah heard Tori sigh. 'Look, Sas, I'm willing to bet that Ben loves his kid—enough to put her before anyone else if he has to—'

'I would hope so!'

'Don't interrupt,' Tori ordered. 'Put yourself in his shoes. What if someone who said they liked you— practically *admitted* they were in love with you—met your kid and then took off to another country?'

Sarah was silent. This *was* a new direction from which to approach the situation.

'It would spell rejection, wouldn't it?' Tori persisted. 'He was already less than impressed that you tried to hand him on to me, wasn't he?'

'I guess…'

'So here's your chance to show him you're actually serious. You *are* serious, aren't you?'

'I guess.'

'Sas!'

'OK. Yes, I'm in love with him, dammit!'

'So hang in there. Wait for a chance to talk to him.'

'I might not get one.'

'Well, you certainly won't if you come home on the next plane. Go and find that doctor in charge and tell him you'll stay. Ask him to let you work with Ben.'

'I couldn't do that!'

'Sas!' Tori's tone was a warning and Sarah grinned.

'OK. I'll stay but I'm not going to chase him around operating theatres. Hey, my battery's getting low. We've been talking for ages.'

'You needed sorting out.'

'How are you, though? Is your leg really feeling that much better?'

'It's great. I'm going to get this brace off in no time and then you won't see me for dust. Guess what I'm planning to do to celebrate?'

But Sarah couldn't guess. Couldn't say a word, in fact.

'Sas? You still there?'

'I have to go,' Sarah whispered urgently. 'I've just seen Ben. He's in the gardens. He's...'

He was coming in her direction.

'Talk to you later.' Sarah snapped her phone shut and took a very deep breath.

Ben was still coming in her direction. Did he know she was sitting here? Had he *seen* her?

Ben had seen the still figure on the bench from the window of Phoebe's second-floor room when he'd gone back to find the toy they had overlooked. The small teddy bear had been stuffed unceremoniously into his pocket as he'd raced down the stairs and through an emergency exit.

He had intended finding Sarah and this was the perfect opportunity. After their last encounter Ben would have been less than surprised if she had refused to speak to him privately, and any chance to offer some sort of apology could well have evaporated if she had been with her colleagues from the relief medical team.

It was ridiculous to feel this nervous about approaching her. She'd been talking on her phone, and the way she had snapped it shut and appeared to be waiting for him only served to increase his apprehension. Whatever was about to happen was important. Maybe too important.

'Mind if I join you?'

Sarah's smile looked as tentative as his had been. 'I didn't think I'd see you again. I thought you were taking Phoebe back to your island.'

'I did. She's safely tucked up in her own bed and probably sound asleep right now. I had to come back.'

'To see a patient?'

'No.' Ben ignored the excuse he could have made about retrieving the beloved teddy bear. That hadn't been the real reason, had it? 'I came back to see you.'

The silence was deafening for several long seconds but the glance that passed between Ben and Sarah spoke volumes. It gave Ben more than enough courage to say what he wanted to say.

'I couldn't leave things like that. I couldn't stop thinking about what you said. About it being me that had the disability rather than Phoebe.'

Even in the dim glow provided by the pathway lights, Ben could see the flush of colour staining Sarah's cheeks.

'You weren't meant to hear that.'

'I'm kind of glad I did. When I stopped fuming long enough to ask myself why I was so angry with you, I realised there was some truth in it.'

'Ben...' Sarah's teeth caught her bottom lip. 'I didn't mean—'

Touching her hand was enough to interrupt but Ben couldn't leave it at that. His fingers slid over hers and caught her hand to cradle it in his own.

'It's not the whole truth, of course. Phoebe leads a very normal life in London. She goes to pre-school, we go out shopping and to places like the zoo at the weekends. She gets stared at and pointed at. She gets kids that call her ''freak'' or ''Gollum'' and you're right—she doesn't understand and it's only just beginning to bother her. *I'm* the one who hates it.'

His thumb was tracing small circles over the base of her wrist now. He could feel the beat of her heart increase as her fingers tightened around his. The tiny squeeze conveyed understanding far more than words could have.

'But here,' Ben continued softly, 'we've found a magic place. We have real time together. We swim and play and hunt for shells. The island women I employ adore Phoebe. It's been a refuge. A place to come when she's recuperating between surgeries. A place we can live together as though there was nothing in the world ready to hurt us.'

A sigh escaped unintentionally but it earned another gentle squeeze from Sarah's hand as encouragement to keep talking.

'I know it can't last,' he admitted. He kept his eyes lowered, staring at the shape their joined hands were making. 'Phoebe will have to start real school. She's going to have to develop the skills and fortitude to cope with what the world will throw at her. I know I could be doing her a disservice by continuing the fantasy but it's only for three months of every year and I'd go mad if we couldn't escape London.'

'You're not happy there?' The sound of Sarah's voice was as comforting as the warmth of her hand.

'Neither of us are. Phoebe associates it with hospital admissions and pain. I have to struggle with commuting for hours on top of work commitments that mean I hardly see my daughter.' He raised his gaze to smile at Sarah.

'You might not believe this, but I made some enquiries about emigrating to New Zealand last year. It seemed like the perfect compromise between a life in the islands and London. I thought we could move after the next lot of surgery. That would still be before Phoebe turns five and has to start school.'

'How much more surgery does she need to have?'

'This will be the last lot for a while. There's a plastic surgeon in London who specialises in facial work. He uses skin extension by inflating saline pouches under normal skin. Phoebe's got enough of an area on her head and neck to expand and use to cover her scars and even replace her hair. It would make a dramatic difference to the way she looks and I think I owe it to her to try.'

He owed it to Phoebe? The guilt and self-blame behind those words explained a lot to Sarah about his over-protectiveness. But it didn't tell her enough about the barrier it created for her. Something Tori had said—about the possibility that Phoebe had been badly treated in the past—surfaced, and the fact that Ben had told her so much already, combined with the link she had with him through the touch of his hand, was enough to make Sarah feel brave.

'What happened to Phoebe, Ben? How did she get burnt?'

He was silent for so long that Sarah decided she'd made a mistake, pushing herself into such personal territory. When he pulled his hand away from hers and used it to rub his forehead as though in unexpected pain, she wished desperately that she had kept her mouth shut. The words Ben spoke sounded harsh.

'It was my fault.'

'I don't believe that.' Sarah reached up and touched Ben's cheek with her fingers. 'I could never believe that.'

'It's true.'

Sarah shook her head. 'No. You tried to hide who you really are from me when we first met, Ben. Just like you hid Phoebe. You were quite convincing but not convincing enough, or I would have been able to forget you when I went home. I've seen a lot more of who you really are in the last two days and nothing would make me believe that you would deliberately harm anyone. Especially a child.'

'You don't know the story.'

'I'm listening,' Sarah said quietly. 'If you want to tell me.'

Ben looked at her for a long moment. Something scurried beneath the shrubs in the surrounding garden but it was the only sound to break the silence. They were still alone in the garden. The soft rustle of branches released scent from some tropical flower, frangipani or jasmine perhaps, and the warmth of the perfumed darkness felt like a cradle.

A safe place where secrets could be shared. Sarah was prepared to tell Ben anything he might want to know about her. She *wanted* to tell him. Anything. Everything.

Did he trust her enough to feel the same way?

He seemed to. But Sarah's joy at his willingness to share was quickly eaten away by the sad story.

'My marriage was a disaster,' Ben told her. 'We both knew that within a short period of time but I hung on, trying to make things better. It wasn't until I found she was having an affair with one of my colleagues that I snapped. I walked out and started divorce proceedings. The affair didn't last long and Erin wanted me to come home. She was pregnant but I refused to accept that the baby was mine, even though it was possible.'

Sarah said nothing, not wanting to interrupt the flow of words.

'I made what I thought was a generous offer by way of a settlement but it wasn't enough for Erin. She came to see me at work one day when the baby was three months old. Pushed her way into my office brandishing a DNA test result proving that Phoebe was my child. Her solicitor had come up with the plan of me signing away a percentage of future earnings instead of a lump sum as child support.'

Ben shook his head. 'I was furious. I felt used. All she wanted from me was money and she was using a helpless baby to get what she wanted. We had a row. I claimed the DNA results were inconclusive, which of course they weren't. She took off in a fury, passed a car on her way home and had a head-on crash with a truck coming around a blind corner. Erin was killed instantly.'

His voice caught. 'The first time I ever saw my daughter was when she was lying in Intensive Care in an induced coma because of the level of pain the burns were causing.'

Sarah had to fill the silence this time. 'You weren't driving that car, Ben. It wasn't your fault.'

'You haven't heard the whole story.' Ben's elbows were on his knees and he leaned forward to bury his face in his hands for a moment. 'I was already in another relationship. A rebound thing that had started three months after I left home. The woman made it clear she wanted to marry me. She claimed she loved Phoebe. I felt responsible for Phoebe having no mother as much as I did for her terrible scarring, so I let the relationship go on. I let it go too far.'

Ben's huff was scathing. 'She was using Phoebe to get to me just the way Erin had. I came home early from work one day and found Phoebe taking her first steps. Tottering towards this person that I thought would be a good mother for her, and you know what she did?'

Ben pushed himself to his feet and walked a few jerky steps before turning an anguished gaze towards Sarah. 'She made some sound that expressed her total disgust with this little scarred creature and she pushed her away and said, ''Don't *touch* me!'' I think it was the first time I heard Phoebe cry for a reason other than horrendous physical pain, and I swore that would never happen again.'

'Oh…Ben.' Sarah was on her feet now as well. She went straight towards Ben and simply held out her arms. For a second he felt rigid in her arms and then Sarah felt him shaking and knew that he was crying. In that moment she knew that her love for this man was infinite. If he could only accept it—and love her back—then nothing could destroy what they could have together.

They held each other for what seemed like a very long time. Ben had shared far more than the story of Phoebe's accident. He might realise just how much of his own soul he had bared and Sarah was afraid that it could be enough to make him retreat. Now was not the time to tell him how much she loved him, no matter how badly she wanted to. What she needed to do was to convey her understanding. And her acceptance. And allow him the dignity of choosing how much else he wanted to reveal.

'You should come and live in New Zealand,' she said decisively. 'You'd love it. So would Phoebe.' She drew back far enough to smile encouragingly. 'For the kind of commuting you have to do in London, you could live right out of the city. On a beach even. And a small country school would be a much gentler environment for Phoebe to start her education.' Her smile was rather shy this time. 'We're not a bad crowd down there. Some of us are really quite nice.'

Ben was smiling now as well. His tears had dried but the gaze from those dark eyes suggested he understood exactly what Sarah was offering. His hand cupped her face.

'I doubt there's anyone else quite as special as you, Sarah Mitchell.' He bent his head and touched her lips with his own, but it was a gentle kiss and not intended to inspire passion. 'Are you too tired to talk any more?'

'Of course not.' Sarah was more than prepared to sit and talk to Ben all night. Or for however long it took for them to reach a place of mutual understanding. She had come here to find out how she felt about Ben Dawson and now she knew beyond any shadow of doubt. But it wasn't enough, was it? She also needed to know how he felt about her.

Ben led her back to the bench and they sat down. Much closer this time because Ben's arm drew Sarah to his side and held her there.

'What you said about me having the disability instead of Phoebe wasn't the only thing that stuck in my head. You said something else. Something about knowing what it was like to be different.' Ben's head turned and Sarah looked up to meet the searching gaze. 'I knew you were different the moment I set eyes on you, but it's obviously nothing physical.'

His gaze held a hint of what Sarah had seen just before he'd kissed her last night. A flicker of desire, held in check right now, but with the promise of easy ignition. 'I've seen you in a bikini, remember? You're gorgeous, Sarah.'

'Thanks.' Sarah dipped her head. The memory of lying on the beach as Ben approached for the first time was so distant now it felt like another lifetime.

'And I've wondered—rather a lot, in fact—over the last month what your life was like before you went to live with Tori's family. Whether that was what made you so different.' Ben cupped her chin to lift her face gently and catch her gaze. 'Did someone hurt you, Sarah?'

Her nod was slow, cradled by Ben's hand.

'Men?'

Sarah nodded again.

'Physical abuse?' A raw anger echoed around the words but then Ben's face tightened and the next word came out in a hoarse whisper. *'Sexual?'*

Sarah shook her head this time. 'Just physical and…emotional, I guess. I never felt wanted and I've never really been able to trust that a man would want me.'

Ben's face was so serious it appeared formidably stern. '*I* want you, Sarah. You know that, don't you?'

Sarah swallowed hard. It was almost too precious a gift to accept. She found herself continuing to talk even as she wondered whether Ben really meant what he'd said. Giving him time to change his mind if he wanted to perhaps.

'I think that's why it worked so well when I finally got placed with Tori's mum, Carol. Her husband had died when Tori was a baby and she'd devoted herself to fostering children to make up the gap in the family. She was especially good with problem kids. The ones with disabilities, either physical or emotional.'

'So that's how you learned to see beneath the scars.'

Sarah nodded, encouraged by Ben's accepting words. 'It saved me. I'd love to do the same for others. *You* were right, too, Ben. I do home in on kids that look like they might be facing rejection. I even…'

'Even what?'

Her smile was shy. But they were sharing secrets here, weren't they? Becoming so much closer.

'I even went to see someone in the social welfare department a little while ago. I wanted to become a foster-mother—like Carol had been. It was Phoebe that gave me the idea, in fact. I found I couldn't forget meeting her.' Sarah held Ben's gaze. 'Maybe it shouldn't be so amazing that she's turned out to be your daughter.'

'Why is that?'

'Because I couldn't forget you either.'

Their gazes held. Locked. A tiny movement from either of them would spark something that might be inappropriate given their potential lack of privacy. Ben cleared his throat.

'Is that what you plan to do when you go home, then? To become a foster-mother?'

'No. They don't want me.'

'Why not? You have a gift with children, Sarah. Even I can see that.'

'I'm too young. And I'm single. I'm not suitable.' Sarah shrugged. The rejection was still disappointing. 'They just don't want me.'

'Good.'

Sarah blinked. 'Good?'

'Yes.' Ben stood up and pulled Sarah to her feet. 'It's good.'

'Why?'

'Because *I* want you.' Ben sounded just as serious as he had the first time he'd made the declaration, but this time something anxious hovered in his words. 'Do you want me, Sarah?'

'More than I can say.'

'Would you come home with me now? To be with me?'

'I'd go anywhere with you. I...I'm in love with you, Ben.'

The sea had calmed as much as the crisis in the island's hospitals had. Ben's powerful boat ate up the distance to his private island and any embarrassment Sarah had felt in collecting her backpack and explain-

ing that she wouldn't be using the team's accommodation that night was left behind on the main island.

It was very late by the time they tied up the boat
and made their way across the beach and up the me-
andering path to Ben's house. A single lamp burned
on the verandah, attracting insects Sarah didn't want
to try and identify. She followed Ben into the house,
up a wide central hallway and then into a bedroom
that looked out over the ocean.

'You must be exhausted,' Ben said. 'There's an *en
suite* bathroom if you'd like a shower.'

Sarah shook her head. What she wanted was standing right in front of her.

Ben understood. He pulled her close and kissed her,
his grip on her shoulders far firmer than the touch of
his lips. Then he pulled away with a soft groan.

'I'm just going to check on Phoebe,' he whispered.
'Be back in a minute.'

In fact, it was less than a minute. Sarah had had
just enough time to shift her backpack and was standing staring at the clean white linen on the vast bed.

Ben took her hand and turned her to face him. 'Are
you sure about this Sarah?'

She could only nod, her mouth suddenly too dry to
speak. She tried to dampen her lips and something
flared in Ben's eyes. Without another word he covered her lips with his own and Sarah was instantly
taken back to where they'd been last night. And the
night of the village celebration. Drawn irresistibly
into a physical desire that brooked no hesitation or
inhibition.

Sarah helped Ben undress as eagerly as she let him
remove her own clothes. She wanted to touch…and
taste his whole body. She wanted to give something

of herself she had never given any man and with Ben it was so easy. Every caress from his fingers or lips drew her closer. She loved the smell of his skin, the solid weight of his body, the silky slide of his tongue against hers.

Never before had Sarah had this sensation of more than a physical union. When she finally felt the piercing satisfaction of Ben entering her body, it was far more than physical release. For a moment suspended in time they became one being and Sarah knew she had found something far too precious to lose.

She lay in Ben's arms later, trying to recapture that moment again and again. It was there but each time she called it back it seemed fainter. The gentle kisses Ben pressed against her head as he settled her to sleep in the crook of his arm, even the soft words of love he spoke, had some kind of static interfering with her trusting their truth.

Sarah couldn't identify what was wrong. She only knew that a faint, very faint, alarm bell was sounding.

Ben held Sarah in his arms. He could feel the soft weight of her breast against his chest. The beat of her heart finally slowing after spent passion. The kisses he pressed into the soft tumble of her dark hair were a compromise he was forcing himself to make. It would be so easy to keep this woman awake, to make love to her again and again, but she needed rest.

So did he. So much had happened tonight. So much had been revealed. Too much? Was that why Ben felt this nagging seed of doubt? He didn't want to try and identify what was causing his unease. He was with the woman he loved far more than he had thought it was possible to love anyone. He never wanted to let her go.

It was best not to try and allow anything to spoil this sense of utter perfection of having Sarah in his bed. In his life. Maybe that seed of doubt was caused simply by the fact that they had had so little time together as yet. He would do something about that. He would delay his return to London and hope that Sarah could take more time away from her own life. They could spend the time they needed to be together on this island sanctuary.

The time they needed to know that it *was* as perfect as it seemed. That they were meant for each other. Soul mates. Destined to be together for the rest of their lives.

Ben's arm tightened imperceptibly around Sarah. As though he knew it couldn't last. That something had to ruin its perfection—the way the flames from burning fuel had damaged his daughter's beauty.

CHAPTER TEN

DOUBTS could be cast aside with remarkable ease when you were living in paradise.

Any lingering trace of unsettled weather vanished on that first night Sarah spent in Ben's arms and she woke to the view of a cloudless sunrise over a magical portion of the Pacific Ocean. The genuine delight on Phoebe's face at finding Sarah in the house was the icing on a cake Sarah had never dreamt of being lucky enough to find.

'It's too good to be true.'

'Oh, rot!' Tori made her fears sound ridiculous. 'It's exactly right for you, Sas. I hope Ben realises how lucky he is.'

'He seems to.' Sarah smiled as she watched several tiny lizards scuttle up the trunk of the coconut palm beside the one she was leaning on. 'I keep finding him staring at me as though *he* thinks it's too good to be true as well.'

'Where is he now?'

'He's gone to the hospital again. He wants to follow up his own cases for the rest of the week and be available for any serious emergencies, but they don't need me any more. I didn't have much to do at all when I went back in with him yesterday.'

'They were fine at work about you taking the extra time. It's coming out of your annual leave, though.'

'That's cool.' It wouldn't have mattered to Sarah

if they'd fired her for telling them she wasn't coming home as soon as expected. She was gathering the ingredients for a new life right now. One that totally eclipsed anything she had ever envisaged having the joy of living.

'What time is it for you now?' Tori queried. 'What are you doing?'

'Just sitting admiring the view,' Sarah responded. 'Waiting for Ben to get back. It's two o'clock. Phoebe's having a nap.'

'What's it like, being on a private island? I didn't get to see too much of it when I was there.'

'Not for lack of trying.' Sarah laughed. 'But we won't go there. The house is gorgeous. Very open and airy, with the most amazing views from almost every room. There's a swimming pool and a track through the garden and the trees all the way to that beach where you broke your leg. Did you see that waterfall there?'

'Yeah. It was beautiful.'

Sarah had stood beside the rocky pool at the base of that waterfall last night. Hand in hand with the man she loved.

'I think it's the most romantic spot on earth,' she murmured.

'Beach wedding, then, huh?'

Sarah bit her lip. She wasn't going to tempt fate by even talking about it. Especially when it reminded her of that curious disappointment after Ben had kissed her so tenderly—and thoroughly—as they'd stood beside that pool. If he *was* thinking in terms of permanence, as she was, it would have been the perfect place and moment to propose. Or, at the very least, to talk about it.

He had been on the verge of saying something, she knew he had. And Sarah had waited, heart pounding, for the words she wanted to hear so much. But Ben had said nothing. He'd broken the eye contact that seemed to be touching Sarah's soul and his smile had been almost poignant as he'd led her away to continue their sunset walk around the island.

As though he knew what she'd been hoping for.

As though he knew he couldn't give it to her.

Fortunately, Tori was in too much of a hurry to pursue the topic. 'I have to go, Sas, or I'll be late for work.' Sarah heard a heartfelt sigh. 'Boy, do I wish I was in *your* shoes.'

Sarah groaned. 'You don't mean you still fancy Ben, I hope?'

'Good grief, no. I would have had him gift-wrapped for you the first day I saw him, you know that. I hope *he* knows that now!'

Sarah was nodding slowly as she spoke. 'It was part of another life as far as Ben's concerned. I think I'm the first person in a very long time to get close to the real Ben.'

'Thank goodness for that. I wouldn't want to be permanently blushing when I'm acting as your bridesmaid. Might look sunburnt or something.' Tori's laugh sounded relieved. 'I just meant that it's pouring with rain here. I think we're getting the tail end of that cyclone.'

'Bad luck.' Sarah tried to sound sympathetic but couldn't keep it up. 'I'll think of you when I take Phoebe down to the beach for her swim this afternoon.'

A group of parrots took fright as Ben's long stride swiftly covered the track that led to the sheltered cove. The flash of brilliant, dark green feathers and the outraged squawking made him slow his step. What was the hurry after all?

He'd only been away for a few hours and he knew that Sarah and Phoebe would be waiting for him. They'd all have another swim, playing in the shallows with his small daughter or taking her for an exciting ride on an adult's back into the lure of deep water.

They would wander back to the house slowly, taking the time to see the beauty of their surroundings through the eyes of a child and stopping whenever necessary to collect some more treasure, like a pretty flower or shell. They had found a baby turtle yesterday and now it was living in a tiny pond in the garden where Phoebe could feed it raw mince. The couple who acted as housekeeper and gardener, living in a bure away from the house, had promised to look after the new pet when the Dawsons went back to London.

Not that Ben or Phoebe had any desire to leave. Especially now that they had Sarah to share their paradise. Even London would become a sunnier and happier place if Sarah came with them. And she would come, if he asked. Ben's stride slowed even more as he reached the outcrop of rocks where Tori had broken her leg that day. He stopped completely as he gained a view of the beach and could see Sarah and Phoebe. They were both standing in the rock pool, holding their hands beneath the heavy shower of the small waterfall, and he could hear Phoebe's gurgling laughter quite clearly.

The dark rocks of the pool and the vibrant greenery of the ferns surrounding it were festooned with jewels of colour from tropical flowers. With the backdrop of pure white sand and the sparkling turquoise of the ocean, it had been the attribute that had sold the island for Ben. He'd never thought of it as being such a romantic place until last night, but right now he could actually see it being the perfect setting for a wedding.

His wedding. To Sarah.

What had stopped him, last night? Dried up those words of commitment—a proposal even? They had been tumbling in his head, eager for release. He had desperately wanted to ask Sarah to share his life. To marry him and…and to be a mother to Phoebe.

And that was precisely what had stopped him.

He'd had the feeling all along that this had been too good to be true. He loved Sarah with a passion that was frightening in its potential to destroy him if he lost it. He didn't have to lose it, though, did he? Sarah apparently loved him just as much. The obstacle of having a child who, to outward appearances, was less than perfect didn't exist with Sarah because she loved Phoebe.

She had a gift with children. A natural affinity with any child who might be facing difficulties in life. She had been prepared to devote her life to such children, and that was what had stopped Ben proposing to her.

It was crazy. The last serious relationship Ben had had with a woman had been terminated because she hadn't loved or even accepted his daughter. Now he'd found someone at the other end of the spectrum totally.

Was he jealous of the bond Sarah had formed with Phoebe over the last few days? The secret looks they shared or the time they spent together? The hand-holding and cuddles?

No. The sight of them together had moved Ben

almost to tears on more than one occasion. Sarah could give Phoebe what was missing in her life. She could give him what was missing in *his* life. But would it be Ben making Sarah's life as happy as it could be?

Or would it be his daughter?

He knew Sarah would have said yes without hesitation if he'd proposed by the waterfall last night, but would she have been saying yes in order to be with him above anything else, or would the attraction of being Phoebe's mother be the main draw card?

It shouldn't actually matter, given that Phoebe had, until now, been the most important person in Ben's life. But he'd been used by women in the past and they had used Phoebe to get to him. An unborn Phoebe to try and make him return to a marriage that had been a disaster. A helpless, newborn Phoebe to try and extract a lifetime financial commitment. A scarred and vulnerable toddler when the pretence of acceptance and love could have made her life intolerable if he'd gone down that particular road any further.

No one could suggest that Sarah was using Phoebe to get to Ben.

But was she using Ben to get to Phoebe?

It shouldn't matter, Ben told himself again, but his feet were still rooted to that spot on the rocks as that seed of doubt finally blossomed into recognition.

Even if it *was* Sarah's desire to be a foster-mother that was bringing them together, he loved her enough to accept whatever love she could spare for him. Judging from the last few days, her supply of love was infinite.

Maybe he was just wishing for the moon. How

could he possibly know if Sarah would have felt the same way if Phoebe hadn't existed? She did exist and the fact that Sarah was in love with his daughter as well as himself should make this perfect.

And it was perfect. And he would propose. He just needed a little more time to get his head around what had to be simply a selfish reaction. Ben unclenched the fists he hadn't known he'd made as he stood there on the rocks. It wasn't that easy to let go of the tension, however, and he decided he wouldn't join Sarah and Phoebe on the beach after all. They might both sense that tension and he didn't want to worry either of them.

He'd jog back along the track and then go for a hard swim on the jetty side of the island. By the time Sarah and Phoebe returned to the house, he would have crushed his doubts. When they had eaten their dinner and Phoebe was tucked up in her bed, he would take Sarah for another walk to the pool.

And this time he would ask her to marry him.

Why had he gone away?

The joy of being with Phoebe, playing under the spray of the waterfall, evaporated for Sarah. Something wasn't right. Something hadn't been quite right all along. She had just refused to allow that niggling doubt to take on any significance.

But she had seen the figure on the rocks, watching them, and Sarah had known she had been under some kind of assessment. He had watched her play with his daughter and if she'd been close enough to see his face she knew she would have caught that odd expression again. The 'too good to be true' look.

Phoebe was everything to her father. Ben had made

that very clear by his protectiveness. He had discarded his last serious relationship because the woman had not accepted or loved Phoebe. He had set up a double life almost, where he could have the occasional fling that could never harm his child. And here Sarah was, prepared to love them both. Prepared to spend the rest of her life loving them both. Knowing that she would be loved back.

Would Ben have felt the same way if he hadn't been a father? Was it *her* he wanted to have in his life, more than any other potential partner? Or was a suitable mother for Phoebe even more important? Ben had admitted he felt guilty about the accident. About Phoebe not having a mother. He'd set out to replace her once before, hadn't he?

Maybe these few days on the island were a test and that was why Phoebe's nanny had been given time off. Ben would propose when he was sure she was the right mother for his child. He must have thought he hadn't been seen, standing on those rocks. Certainly Phoebe hadn't spotted her father and Sarah had pretended not to have seen him, allowing herself to secretly enjoy the anticipation of him coming closer.

Had he expected to see her push Phoebe away? Or give some other hint that her love for the little girl was a ruse? He couldn't have seen anything that might have bothered him. Phoebe had a dry dressing over her sutures and they had agreed that a bathe in salt water and even a little sunshine would speed the healing of her wound. She had on a long-sleeved shirt covering her scarred arm, and the sunhat with the veil protecting the grafted skin from sunburn. And she'd been laughing—clearly happy in Sarah's company. As she had been from the moment Sarah had joined them in their private hide-away.

So why had he gone away?

Maybe his phone had summoned him to an emergency. Maybe he had been talking to someone as he'd stood there on the rocks. There was nothing to worry about. Sarah smiled at Phoebe.

'Time we went home, sweetheart.'

'But Daddy hasn't come for a swim.'

'He might be busy. We need to go and feed your turtle, don't we?'

'OK.'

'You haven't got a name for him yet. Shall we try and think of one while we walk back to the house?'

'You think of one,' Phoebe commanded.

'Is is a girl or a boy, do you think?'

'A girl,' Phoebe decided firmly. 'Like Phoebe.'

'How 'bout we call her Michelle, then? 'Cos she's got a very pretty shell, hasn't she?'

Phoebe sighed happily and held up her arms. 'I want to go and feed Shell.'

Sarah picked her up and started to walk back towards the start of the track near the rocks where Ben had been standing.

She had nothing to worry about. She would pass any test concerning Phoebe that Ben might want to put to her. And if Ben *did* want her as a mother more than simply for herself, did it really matter? She would still agree to marry him because even if it was a shade less than perfect, it was still far more than she could have dreamt of.

They would still be together and her love for Ben

was so great that she could make it work. Love was never perfectly equal on both sides, was it? That was the stuff of fairy-tales, not real life.

The call that came from the hospital as they were eating dinner that night seemed to bother Ben considerably.

'I'm sorry about this, but I'll have to go in again.'

'It's not Atekini, is it?' Sarah asked anxiously. 'He hasn't developed peritonitis from that branch spearing his abdomen, has he?'

'No. We were lucky there. The antibiotic cover was enough to prevent any nasty complications. His knee is healing beautifully, too, though I don't think he'll be able to realise his dream of playing rugby for Fiji.'

'Don't go, Daddy,' Phoebe pleaded. 'I want a story.'

'I have to go, pumpkin. Somebody's had an accident on their motorbike and they've broken lots of bones.' Ben tousled the soft blonde curls. 'Maybe Sarah could read your story tonight.'

'I'd love to read your story.' Sarah nodded. 'We could have the one about Yertle the turtle again.' She caught Ben's gaze. 'You'll be gone for a while by the sound of it.'

He nodded. 'Don't wait up for me. I might have to stay all night.'

His dark brown eyes conveyed just how much he would miss the love-making they would have shared. How much he would miss being with Sarah while Phoebe was asleep and they had precious hours of simply being with each other. Sarah sent back the message that she would miss those hours just as much. Then she smiled. Everything *would* be all right, she just knew it would.

'Be careful out there. We'll be fine until you get back.'

Dawn broke to herald another perfect day, but Ben hadn't returned from the hospital. The housekeeper, Mara, served breakfast by the pool and relayed the message that Ben would be home by lunchtime. Sarah smiled at Phoebe.

'We'll find something nice to do this morning before it gets too hot. Shall we go and pick some flowers and make a lei for Daddy?'

But Phoebe was distracted when they reached the beach beside the jetty.

'I want to go on the boat.'

'Daddy's got the boat. He needs it to come home.'

'The other boat.' Phoebe was pointing beneath the jetty, where one of the type of boats Sarah had seen in the islands was pulled up onto the sand. It was wooden and flat, rather like a squared canoe, and it had a sturdy-looking paddle resting in its base.

'Why not?' Sarah wondered aloud. The sea was as calm as it had been the day she had swum to one of the islands near the resort. Phoebe was well covered and the sun wasn't at its strongest yet. A ride around the island would fill in some time and maybe when they got back Ben would have returned.

It was easy enough to launch the small boat through the gentle surf. Phoebe sat in the centre of its base, laughing with delight as the waves rocked her. She squealed in excitement as the low-lying vessel tipped when Sarah climbed aboard and then she settled back to enjoy the ride. Sarah took the boat far enough away from the island to make sure they didn't snag any rocks on the other side and once she got used to the heavy paddle they cut across the glistening water with an easy smoothness.

'I can see *fish*,' Phoebe shouted.

They floated for a while, admiring the clarity of the water and the wealth of aquatic life on display.

'Make the boat go fast,' Phoebe commanded finally.

Sarah grinned. 'Hold on tight, then. Here we go.'

'I can see a *big* fish,' Phoebe shouted a few minutes later. 'Look, Sarah!'

Sarah slowed her vigorous paddling and turned to look.

'Oh, my God,' she breathed in horror.

In her attempt to provide Phoebe with the fast boat ride, she had taken no notice of the direction in which they had travelled. Straight out to sea, in fact. They were now much further away from the hilly outlines of Ben's island than she was happy about.

It wouldn't have been a problem, except that the 'big fish' Phoebe had spotted had a triangular black fin.

Sharks didn't attack for no reason, Sarah reminded herself. How many times had she told Tori that her fears were based on a myth perpetuated by gruesome horror movies?

And how many times had Tori countered her reassurance by triumphantly recalling well-publicised incidents of hapless swimmers who had lived the nightmare of just such attacks, with the result of severed limbs or even death?

Sarah pulled the paddle from the water, not wanting to attract the attention of the shark. Surely it would go on its way in a little while and then she could turn the boat around and get Phoebe safely back home.

'It's going round and round,' Phoebe exclaimed. 'That big fish likes us, Sarah.'

The shark wasn't simply circling the small boat. It was getting closer and closer with each circuit.

Desperately, Sarah scanned the horizon. There were a dozen islands nearby. There should be fishing boats out or tourist launches. Yachts or even cruise ships. But there was nothing close. The humps of neighbouring islands were far enough away to appear misty. She and Tori had paddled to Ben's island easily enough but that had been from the other side. Sarah had no idea how far these islands actually were and, without paddling, the boat was being drawn steadily further away from the island she most wanted to get back to.

Ben's island.

A bump on the side of the boat made Sarah gasp but Phoebe's grin was clearly visible through the protection of her veiled hat.

'He wants to play!'

'He's not a nice fish,' Sarah said carefully. 'Stay in the middle of the boat, darling, and try to stay very, very still.'

Sarah knelt closer to the edge. The heavy paddle was a pathetic weapon but it was all she had available, and she had to try and do something. One of Tori's accounts of disaster leapt to mind, where a surfer had had his board bitten in half by a shark. The sides of this small boat wouldn't offer much more in the way of resistance to rows of razor sharp teeth and the power of a fifteen-foot long creature.

If that fragile barrier was broken, both Sarah and Phoebe would be at the mercy of whatever else the primitive animal had in mind, and the thought of Phoebe being mauled was simply unbearable.

She raised the paddle above her head, balancing carefully, waiting for the next circuit that would bring the shark within range.

It came further within range than she had expected. With a powerful surge, the snout broke through the surface of the water, mouth open to suggest vicious intent. Sarah brought the paddle down as hard as she could, the violent rocking of the boat and Phoebe's scream only adding to her terror as the shark's jaws clamped around the paddle, splintering the wood and tearing it from her hands.

She had nothing left to try and protect them with now. Phoebe understood the danger they were in and was now shrieking in terror. And in the end there was only one thing Sarah could do. She crawled into the centre of the boat and pulled Phoebe into her arms, a tiny ball of petrified humanity. She wrapped her sarong tightly around the child to try and make her feel more secure. She bent her head over Phoebe's, her long, dark hair providing an illusion of greater protection.

Then she waited. Drifting with the current. Knowing that, at any second, another attack could come.

Ben didn't ease back on the throttle of his jet boat until he was very close to the jetty of home. He was a man in a hurry. He had to find Sarah and talk to her.

It hadn't been a conversation he could have had over the telephone, which was why he had left a message for Mara to pass on this morning. It was an interchange he wanted to have in a particular place. At the foot of a small waterfall. Sunset would have been perfect but he wasn't going to wait that long.

The fatigue of having been up all night in the operating theatre had been blown away by the wind in his face as he'd pushed his boat to cover the distance to get home. No—the fatigue had been blown away with the realisation that any doubts he'd had about Sarah had been entirely unfounded.

Being in the hospital had finally cleared his mind. Standing in the same scrub room where he had seen Sarah again for the first time since the day of Tori's accident. She had come back to Fiji with the relief medical team partly because she had hoped to see *him* again. She had had no idea he was Phoebe's father.

She had still had no idea that day they had gone on the mission to the outlying island. When they had swum together. When the summons back to shore had been the only thing that had stopped them making love there and then, in the sea. Nothing in that department had changed since she had learned of his daughter's existence.

It *was* him that Sarah wanted above anything else.

Yes, she felt an affinity to children who needed special care, but she had already planned to offer that care to another child—to any child that might need her. It wasn't Phoebe in particular that she wanted, but she was prepared to accept and love her as her own and it was that extra dimension that made her love for Ben perfect.

Not too good to be true.

Just perfect.

Because it *was* an extra dimension. It had been Ben

that Sarah had come back for. Ben that she wanted and loved most of all. He was the luckiest man alive, and if he lost her because he wasn't prepared to trust that love, then he would be the stupidest man alive.

He was going to find her and tell her exactly how he felt. He couldn't wait for the romance of a beach pool in moonlight.

In fact, he couldn't even wait to reach the house. Ben noticed that the island boat was gone from beneath the jetty as he threw the rope to secure his own boat. He looked up to see Mara standing on the deck of the house that overlooked the jetty.

'Sarah?' he yelled. 'In the boat?'

Mara was nodding. She was saying something else but was too far away for Ben to catch the words. He had heard enough anyway. He knew where to find Sarah. She must have taken the boat out to give herself something to do while Phoebe had her nap. She wouldn't be far away and she would be alone.

Maybe a quiet time, being rocked by a gentle ocean under the brilliance of a tropical sun was just as romantic a place to propose. Ben couldn't give a damn. He just wanted to find Sarah and seek the reassurance that she felt the same way. That they would be together for the rest of their lives.

There was no sign of the flat wooden boat when Ben circled his island. He made a wider circuit, feeling his tension spiral. Why would Sarah have gone so far? Had she decided to leave? It was too late to go back and quiz Mara now and Ben was travelling so fast he didn't want to take his hands off the wheel to use his cellphone.

He would find Sarah soon, he knew he would. In fact, wasn't that dark spot on the expanse of the ocean ahead a small craft of some sort?

It was. As Ben roared closer he could see the huddled shape of a figure in its centre and that was when the fear really kicked in. Sarah was in danger.

His own life was in danger.

He saw the fin of the shark as he throttled back, hoping he hadn't misjudged the distance so that the wake of his speeding boat wouldn't overturn Sarah's refuge.

He had to go slowly. To ease his boat carefully in and close the gap. Ready to pull Sarah to safety. Into his arms. The look on her face would have pulled him into the jaws of hell to rescue her.

'Ben! Thank God you're here!'

'Stand up carefully, darling. I don't want you tipping into the water.'

'I think your boat has scared the shark away.'

'I want you safe here with me anyway. Are you ready?'

Sarah nodded, unwrapping her sarong as she prepared to stand up, and it was only at that moment that Ben saw what had been hidden.

'Phoebe!' He was frozen with shock for a split second before he could reach out to take his child.

'I'm so sorry, Ben.' Tears were pouring down Sarah's cheeks now. 'I didn't mean to put Phoebe in danger.'

But Phoebe was safe now. And Ben's arms were outstretched again.

'I know that,' he said softly. 'Come here, Sarah. It's time to go home.'

*   *   *

He hadn't known that Phoebe was in the boat with her. The fear on Ben's face had been purely for Sarah. He would have risked anything to save *her*.

And Sarah knew, as she lay in his arms again that night, that nothing could ever make her doubt any part of Ben's love for her again.

The proposal had been very different from what she had dreamed of. No gentle gurgle of water in a rock pool accompanied it. It had been the roar of a jet boat as Ben had brought them home, Phoebe sandwiched between him and Sarah as he'd held the three of them together.

'I love you, Sarah,' he'd shouted.

'I love you, too, Ben.'

'Marry me?'

'*Yes!* Of course I will.'

'Me, too!' Phoebe had shouted happily. 'Marry *me*, too!'

'You'll be there, pumpkin,' Ben promised.

Sarah had smiled down at the small face. 'You'll be the prettiest flower girl ever.'

Phoebe Dawson *was* the prettiest flower girl ever.

Nearly a year later, after the last major surgery she would ever need and after their life in London had been wrapped up, she stood with her father on the beach of a tiny island in the Pacific beside a rock pool, the edges of which had been festooned with banks of sweet-smelling tropical flowers.

She watched, entranced, as her father and the woman who had just officially become the mother she already loved shared a kiss to mark the end of a simple ceremony and the start of a new life together.

Mummy looked really pretty, Phoebe decided. It

didn't matter that she was a little bit fat because that bump under the folds of the long white dress was going her be her new brother or sister.

They were going to live in a new house near Aunty Tori, and Phoebe was going to go to school. They would still come back to the island for holidays but Phoebe had important things to learn at school and she was going to be a big help in looking after her baby.

It was all so exciting that Phoebe started to feel very impatient. Why on earth did Daddy and Mummy need to have a kiss that was lasting quite *that* long?

MILLS & BOON®

Live the emotion

Medical
romance™

0705/03b

A FAMILY WORTH WAITING FOR

by *Margaret Barker* (French Hospital)

Jacky Manson can't believe it when her new post
at the Hôpital de la Plage brings her face to face
with Pierre Mellanger, the man she has loved ever
since she can remember. At last he sees her for the
beautiful and competent woman she is – but they
both have secrets to reveal…and it's only in the
telling that their lives will take a whole new turn!

IN HIS TENDER CARE by *Joanna Neil*

(A&E Drama)

Sasha Rushford balances an intense career as a
paediatrician with her role as head of the family –
she's used to calling the shots and going it alone. Her
new boss, consultant Matt Benton, soon realises she
is as much in need of saving as the children in their
care – and he's determined to persuade her to accept
the love he wants more than anything to give her.

EARTHQUAKE BABY by *Amy Andrews*

Trapped under a collapsed building, Laura Scott
thought she would never survive. One man kept
her alive and led her to safety – Dr Jack Riley. That
life-saving moment led to a night of unforgettable
intimacy, but it's ten years before they meet again.
Jack soon discovers how real their connection was
– and that Laura is the mother of a ten-year-old
child…

On sale 5th August 2005

*Available at most branches of WHSmith, Tesco, ASDA, Martins,
Borders, Eason, Sainsbury's and all good paperback bookshops*

Visit www.millsandboon.co.uk

4 FREE

BOOKS AND A SURPRISE GIFT!

We would like to take this opportunity to thank you for reading this Mills & Boon® book by offering you the chance to take FOUR more specially selected titles from the Medical Romance™ series absolutely FREE! We're also making this offer to introduce you to the benefits of the Reader Service™—

* ★ FREE home delivery
* ★ FREE gifts and competitions
* ★ FREE monthly Newsletter
* ★ Exclusive Reader Service offers
* ★ Books available before they're in the shops

Accepting these FREE books and gift places you under no obligation to buy, you may cancel at any time, even after receiving your free shipment. Simply complete your details below and return the entire page to the address below. You don't even need a stamp!

YES! Please send me 4 free Medical Romance books and a surprise gift. I understand that unless you hear from me, I will receive 6 superb new titles every month for just £2.75 each, postage and packing free. I am under no obligation to purchase any books and may cancel my subscription at any time. The free books and gift will be mine to keep in any case.

M5ZED

Ms/Mrs/Miss/Mr ....Initials ....
BLOCK CAPITALS PLEASE
Surname ....
Address ....

....

....Postcode..................................

Send this whole page to:
UK: FREEPOST CN81, Croydon, CR9 3WZ